No one writes romantic fiction like Barbara Cartland.

Miss Cartland was originally inspired by the best of the romantic novelists she read as a girl —writers such as Elinor Glyn, Ethel M. Dell and E. M. Hull. Convinced that her own wide audience would also delight in her favorite authors, Barbara Cartland has taken their classic tales of romance and specially adapted them for today's readers.

Bantam is proud to publish these novels—personally selected and edited by Miss Cartland—under the imprint

**BARBARA CARTLAND'S
LIBRARY OF LOVE**

D1431913

Bantam Books by Barbara Cartland
Ask your bookseller for the books you have missed

Barbara Cartland's Library of Love

Barbara Cartland's Library of Love

Ashes of Desire
by Pamela Wynne

Condensed by Barbara Cartland

BANTAM BOOKS · TORONTO · NEW YORK · LONDON

ASHES OF DESIRE
A Bantam Book / June 1978

ISBN 0-553-11815-3

Published simultaneously in the United States and Canada

Bantam Books are published by Bantam Books, Inc. Its trade-
mark, consisting of the words "Bantam Books" and the por-
trayal of a bantam, is registered in the United States Patent
Office and in other countries. Marca Registrada. Bantam
Books, Inc., 666 Fifth Avenue, New York, New York 10019.

PRINTED IN THE UNITED STATES OF AMERICA

Introduction
by
Barbara Cartland

Pamela Wynne wrote this book in the twenties and I find it has a fascinating appeal which has not been lost over the years. Even if slightly incredulous, one is irresistibly drawn to the helpless innocence of Flame and the tangles in which she becomes involved.

Hugh with his passionate, idealistic nature is the right man for her, but one is terrified they will not eventually find happiness together.

Chapter
One

"Good morning, Waterton."

Flame's voice was quite steady as she walked away from the chair which held her twin.

"Isn't it a heavenly day? It's our birthday; did you know, Waterton?"

"Of course I know, Miss Flame. I wish you both a very happy return of the day."

"Thank you, Waterton," Flame answered.

She held up her flower-like face to be kissed.

"I say, Flame!"

Nigel Peterson stood up in his place and made violent signs.

"Why not? I like Waterton far better than anyone else in this house except you. He's been much nicer to me than anyone else, much nicer than you even, because you've had phases of thinking that I was only a girl, and therefore something dreadfully stupid.

"Kiss me, Waterton; I want you to."

"I beg your pardon, Miss Flame." The heavy jowl of the old butler was shaking as he looked down into the blue eyes.

1

"Sir Nigel is right, it would not be seemly. But I thank you, Miss Flame, and I shall remember your kind permission till my dying day."

Placing the coffee-pot and hot milk jug hastily on the table, the old man left the room, groping awkwardly for his handkerchief.

"You *are!*"

Nigel Peterson spoke in a disgusted undertone as he half got out of his chair to reach across the table for the coffee.

"Girls of seventeen don't go cadging about for kisses. Do pull yourself together a bit, and remember that you're practically grown up; a thing like that makes me feel such a fool."

Flame Peterson was still standing by the sideboard, but her face was turned towards the row of silver dishes with their little methylated lamps underneath.

Her soft breast was heaving. She loved Waterton; he was really the only friend she had in the house.

Since her father's death nobody there had really cared for her, and he had only cared for her in patches; besides, that was a long time ago.

Flame knew that her mother did not care for her at all, and that she almost loathed Nigel for the way that Daddy had tied up his money.

So in her really very lonely life with a series of governesses, Waterton had been her constant confidant and friend.

"Why do you grudge me loving Waterton?" she asked.

Her grey eyes were round and desolate.

"I don't. But all I do say is that when you're seventeen you put a stopper on all this free kissing. It's not done, especially to a butler at breakfast-time."

"Eton has made you a disgusting snob."

"No, it hasn't. Anyway, I've got a ripping scheme for today. We'll get old jawbones to put us up some lunch and we'll clear off to the Myne woods. I want to see if I can track down a woodpecker, and I want to photograph it near."

"In a way it's a mercy that Mother never bothers about what we do." Flame smiled.

What's she doing today?" Nigel asked.

"Going up to town to have a fitting."

"Oh, my aunt! Do you think she's going to be married again?"

"Married again! Mother! Who would marry Mother?" Flame asked with wide eyes.

"You silly juggins; heaps of people. Mother's frightfully good-looking."

"Mother good-looking!"

This was something quite new to Flame.

"Yes, and you're the dead spit of her, too," Nigel answered. "You've got that yellow hair and those black eyebrows and eyelashes, and a mouth that looks as if your tooth had been bleeding."

"Nigel!"

"Yes, well, you have. I can't help it." Nigel dropped his eyes to his plate.

"Well, if I've got all those things, so have you," retorted Flame. "We're exactly alike, everyone says so."

"Yes, I know we are, but it's all right for a man. It's for a girl that it's so desperate."

"Well, if I am like that, I can't help it. I think it most frightful of you to tell me like that on my birthday. Besides, you say that Mother's good-looking with all those things, why shouldn't I be too?"

Flame's eyes were miserable and protesting.

"Mother's much taller than you are; that makes it all right."

Nigel Peterson's mouth was twitching with satisfaction under his table napkin. Flame was just at the age when she might get past herself if she realized how very pretty she was.

One or two of his form had got quite potty about her at the Eton and Harrow. And you couldn't have that beginning, because you never knew where it would end.

Nigel, looking at her appraisingly, supposed that it must be her hair: it was bobbed, and yellow, with a sort of funny tawny streak in it in places.

"Come on, let's get out," he said, getting up and scraping his chair back over the polished boards.

Just as they were leaving, their mother appeared and told them not to be late for lunch as she had invited Lord Lovegrove.

"What possesses Mother to ask that greasy old sandbag to lunch?" Nigel wondered. "I thought you said she was going up to town."

"I thought she was. But it must be after lunch she is going, and not before."

They walked for a while in silence, and then suddenly Flame burst out:

"I say, do you know how people have babies?"

"Rather."

"Tell me, then," Flame insisted, wondering why her heart was beating so fast.

"Not I! Ask old Mincemeat," responded Nigel, feeling rather uncomfortable, but determined not to show it.

Besides, Flame must know that surely.

Nigel did not realize how little opportunity a girl who does not go to school has of knowing anything of the kind.

"No, you tell me, Mincemeat is such an old donkey she would probably tell me all wrong."

"Well . . . oh, my gaudy aunt!"

Nigel became very red and blew breathily up to the sky.

"You do ask the most hopeless questions, Flame. What on earth do you want to know now for? Well, if you will have it—you sit on an egg."

He burst out laughing.

"You *don't*." Flame's eyes were indignant. "All right; if you are going to say imbecile things like that, I shall ask Waterton."

"No, you can't," Nigel answered quickly.

"All right then, you tell me."

"Well"—Nigel took a long breath—"you ought to know. That horrible cat of yours, it has kittens about every other day; can't you gather anything from that?"

"What, do we have them like that! What a wretched arrangement!"

Flame's eyes, now quite calm again, were deeply ruminative.

"God ought to have thought of something better. But somehow I thought it was that. Thank you, Nigel. Your ears are all red," she said, chuckling.

"So would yours be if you had a sister like you," said Nigel, deeply ruffled.

Flame was really the outside edge. But, thank Heaven, she appeared to have switched off the subject now. And here were the woods, dark and deeply green against the blue sky.

"Come on and don't make a row. I saw a woodpecker skip round behind that old trunk. Crawl, you fathead!" And Nigel dropped on his knees in the long grass.

Lunch was over, very nice and beautifully served, as it always was, and the twins were stretched on two flowery chesterfield sofas in the library.

It was three o'clock and the long limousine car had just slid away from the front door, carrying in its extremely comfortable embrace their mother and her guest.

"What an old goggler he is!" Nigel exclaimed.

"Yes, isn't he awful?"

"What were you and the old buffer doing for so long in the sunken garden?" Nigel asked.

"Were we long?"

Flame had a wild impulse to put off as long as possible the telling of her twin what had happened. Somehow, she hated the thought of his being angry, angry and disgusted.

"About half an hour."

"Oh, was it as long as that?"

"Quite. What were you doing all the time?"

"Don't make a fuss if I say."

"Try not to."

But Sir Nigel's eyes had suddenly become alert.

"Oh, the old donkey was trying to kiss me."

Flame's little pointed face had suddenly become furtive and ashamed. She dared not look at her brother.

"Was he, though? How very disgusting!"

Nigel Peterson withdrew his eyes from his sister's face and levelled them on an old oil painting that hung over the open fireplace. He had suspected as much; there had been something in his mother's expression when they got up from lunch that had made him suspicious.

"Take Lord Lovegrove down to the sunken garden to see the delphiniums, darling," she had said.

Lady Peterson never said "darling" to her children unless there was some reason for it.

Nigel felt a fierce stirring of anger within him. That doddering old fool and his pretty little sister. Disgusting! But it was quite likely to be her game.

The old beast had pots of money, and their estates adjoined.

"I hope you smacked his ugly face for him," he said violently.

"No, I didn't. How could I? He made me afraid," Flame replied miserably. "Besides, he started off by saying that Mother thought that it would be so nice if I could get to like ..."

She gave a little sob and went on.

"He said something about how my hair shone in the sunlight ... at least, I think he did. And then he put out his arm, and somehow his face seemed to gleam, and I tried to push it away."

Her voice sharpened.

"He loomed over me, you could almost see the kiss frothing on his mouth; so I put my head up suddenly and the back of it hit his chin. He was fearfully sick; a hit like that hurts like anything."

"Good for you! Hope the old beast takes the hint." Nigel laughed joyfully.

But Flame's eyes were brooding and gloomy.

"If Mother once gets the idea into her head that it would be nice for me to marry him, I'm done. You know what Mother is if she once makes up her mind about anything."

"Look here, Flame," Nigel said after a moment, and his sister raised her yellow head with a start.

Nigel's voice wasn't a bit as it generally was.

"Look here, Flame, don't be futile over this. Being married isn't the sort of thing to joke about. Remember, you're grown up. No one can make you marry that old beast unless you give in like a silly idiot."

"Mother could." Flame's voice was melancholy.

"No, she couldn't."

"I tell you she could," Flame answered vehemently. "Nigel, being at Eton has made you forget what Mother is really like, or perhaps she's got more like it, because she is older . . . I don't know . . . She's got that sort of way that *makes* you."

"Rubbish!"

But in spite of the scoffing rejoinder, Sir Nigel had got off the flowery sofa and was walking up and down the polished boards, slipping each foot in turn along in front of him.

Flame was right, and he knew she was. His mother had that compelling way with her.

"Don't be a silly juggins," he said impatiently. "I can't go back to school if you're going to be futile like this."

"What am I to do, then?" said Flame, very near to tears.

"Smack the old pig's face if he comes too near you, and if things get really bad, send me a wire."

"Will you come if I send you a wire?" breathed Flame.

"Yes, I will. But if I find out that you've sent me a wire for any potty reason, I'll flay you alive," Nigel Peterson replied.

"How bad must they be, then, before I send you a wire?" inquired Flame, her lower lip quivering.

"As bad as this: that the old goggler has asked you to marry him, that you have said you won't, and that Mother has said that you are to," replied her brother.

"All right," said Flame. As she looked up at her brother her small face was all aglow with love and admiration.

Flame paced up and down her room. Lunch was just over, lunch for four people: her mother, Colonel Forsythe, Lord Lovegrove, and herself.

She had made the excuse that she wanted to find some snapshots of Eton to show Lord Lovegrove; she had found them at once, but she had not yet started to go downstairs again.

Was it time to send a telegram to Nigel, or was it not? That was the question that was racking her brain to the exclusion of everything else. Lord Lovegrove had not yet proposed in so many words, but he might at any moment.

Her mother had made her put on a softly revealing little frock, and even Gerald Forsythe was

disgusted to see the way in which the self-indul-
gent old face gloated over the childish curves.

"You're selling that child, Phil," he said a
few minutes later.

Flame was crossing the lawn with lagging
feet. She had come down from her room; what
was the good of trying to stay in it? Her mother
would only send for her. . . .

"No, I'm not."

Lady Peterson spoke swiftly and hotly. If
Gerald began to suspect her, she was lost.

Gerald, the only man who had stirred her
pulses an iota, Gerald, the man who made her feel
like a whipped child, the man who with lifted
finger could make her do anything. . . .

"Now then . . ." Colonel Forsythe spoke
warningly, and turned from the window.

"Gerald!" The beautiful face was broken up
and quivering.

"Very well, then; behave!" Colonel Forsythe
turned his gaze to the lawn again.

Lord Lovegrove had got up from the low
chair and was walking to meet the lagging figure.

"I say you are selling the child," he repeated;
"you can see the old beast means to have her, and
she obviously loathes the sight of him."

"Gerald!"

"Don't say it again, it bores me!" Colonel
Forsythe turned finally from the window and held
out a careless hand.

"Come over here, and tell me what you have
been doing with your totally unscrupulous self
since I saw you last."

"I won't come!" Lady Peterson was holding her
white hands clenched against her neck and was
staring over them.

"Very well, then stay where you are," Colonel Forsythe replied.

He crossed one gaitered leg over the other, and dropped his amused and rather cruel eyes on to the cigarette that he was tapping against the arm of the chair.

"Gerald, I want to come." Lady Peterson's voice came haltingly, like a child's.

"Very well, then, come, but don't make such a song about it."

Although Colonel Forsythe spoke brutally, his eyes were full of suppressed passion.

She was heavenly beautiful, this woman of his. But she was of the type that must be kept to heel, otherwise the relationship meant slavery. At fifty, you cannot begin to be a slave.

In the big thatched summer-house, Flame was sitting in the scarlet-cushioned seat, her knees tightly pressed together.

"But I don't like you in that way," she was saying feverishly.

"What way, darling?" Lord Lovegrove was fifty-eight, and he looked it.

"Why, the sort of way that one ought to like a husband."

"And what is that?" inquired Lord Lovegrove, his sensual mouth all aquiver.

"Why, something like I feel for Nigel, only not quite, because he is my brother," said Flame with a sort of flushed hurriedness.

"Ah . . ." Lord Lovegrove got up and walked to the door of the summer-house. "All those feelings would come," he said huskily.

"Are you sure?" queried Flame doubtfully.

But although she spoke doubtfully, her spirits rose a little. What a solution of the whole affair if she could marry this man without minding too much! Freedom from the tyranny of her mother!

A chance to travel about. Lord Lovegrove was always going off somewhere; a chance to have Nigel to stay with his friends, and to give them a heavenly time.

Flame raised her head.

At the sight of that little face, set like an anemone on a slim stalk, Lord Lovegrove made the mistake of his life and lost his self-control.

"Let me go! . . ." Flame was fighting like a fly that feels the tentacles of a spider. "Let me go, I tell you, I loathe your holding me! Let me go! Oh, you pig, you pig! Stop kissing me . . ."

Flame was beating at the padded shoulders with clenched fists. But Lord Lovegrove was still a good deal stronger than Flame.

He did not let her go until the little scarlet mouth was bruised and flaming.

Then he staggered back against the varnished walls of the summer-house, his breath coming very heavily.

Flame was weeping into her clenched fists.

"Pig, pig!" she wept. "Pig, I would rather be dead than marry you. Oh, how I wish my brother was here! He would help me to kill you. How dare you kiss me, you've made me unclean now and for ever."

With one more wild lurch with a clenched fist Flame dashed out of the summer-house, and fled, wailing under her breath, across the velvety lawn that she had crossed so slowly a few minutes before.

Two people saw the stormy return: Colonel

Forsythe for one, lounging in the bay-window of the library, an excellent cigar between his equally excellent teeth; and Waterton for the other, stretched at full length in a padded wicker chair in the window of the stillroom.

Waterton's exclamation was the more expressive:

"I thought as much!"

He half got up, and then sat down again.

"What's that?" Mrs Bullock, the housekeeper, raised her eyes from her book, leaving a well pricked finger in between the pages as she did so.

"Why, it's that Lovegrove. After our Miss Flame, or my name's not Waterton."

"She'd never go as far as that!"

Mrs Bullock forgot that she was keeping a place with her finger, and let both hands fall on to the arms of her chair.

"Wouldn't she? She'd do anything to keep the place clear for her Gerald."

Waterton got up and began to pace about the room.

"Hear that side door?" he continued, one side of his pale face raised a little. "Don't tell me that our Miss Flame'd charge into the house like that for nothing."

"But the man's three times her age!"

Mrs Bullock's round face was incredulous.

She did not like Lady Peterson any more than Waterton did, but she credited her with some semblance of decent feeling.

But Waterton waited at meals, and took in coffee, and had once or twice been in the back drawing-room when Lady Peterson had not known he was there, so decent feelings and the lady of the house were not coupled together in his mind.

"Three times her age! She'd marry her to a man eight times her age if it suited her purpose," returned Waterton viciously.

His old heart ached for the child who was dashing along the corridor just above their heads.

Gerald Forsythe roused himself sufficiently to get up, cross the room, and open the door just a crack to see what Flame looked like when she passed through the wide hall.

He whistled through his lower teeth as he saw the streaming eyes and the scarlet patches round the little red mouth.

Phillida was going too far in this affair. He shut the door cautiously and went back to his seat in the window.

After all, as he meditated, rolling his cigar from one corner of his mouth to the other, what was her game?

Flame was a beautiful little creature and would be certain to marry without any difficulty. Why try to hustle her off the stocks like this?

Then a probable solution of the mystery dawned on him. He threw back his bull-dog head and grinned with his two rows of bull-dog teeth.

She was jealous, that woman of his! Jealous of him and that baby. Pah!

Meanwhile Flame at her big crystal wash-hand basin was swishing water over her face with frantic squeezings of the sponge.

She would wire to Nigel . . . she would *go* to Nigel!

But how could she ever face Nigel after this? Although, of course, she need not let him know the true horror of the whole thing.

But he would find out, something would show it in her face, that that horrible mouth had been squashed against hers.

Flame rushed, all dripping, to the glass and stared wildly into it. Yes, she didn't look the same, there were red marks all round her lips, and one place was turning bluey. Supposing it never got right again!

Or supposing . . .

At that awful unspeakable thought Flame staggered back from the glass and dropped white and trembling into a chair.

Supposing that she had a baby! How else? You loved a man and he kissed you. You didn't kiss a man unless you were going to marry him, and when you did marry a man you almost always had a baby.

"Lord, help me!"

Flame began to rush up and down the room, mad with fear. Whom could she ask? No one! Anyone would shrink from her in disgust and horror at what had just taken place.

"I can't live . . . I can't live!" Flame moaned, and clenching her hands she rushed to her bed and flung herself face downwards on it.

Her life was settled for good then, she would have to marry Lord Lovegrove!

Flame sank slowly back on to her face and buried her wet forehead in the down pillow, with its beautiful monogrammed pillow-case.

"Well, what is all this about?"

As Lady Peterson came slowly over the floor towards the bed, Flame started at the sound of a closing door. She met her mother's hard eyes.

"I didn't feel frightfully well, so I came up to

lie down," said Flame, groping in her sleeve for her handkerchief.

"Really! It has come on very suddenly."

Lady Peterson reached out for a low wicker chair and began to drag it nearer to the bed.

"Don't lie to me, Flame," she said. "I know exactly what has happened. Lord Lovegrove has proposed to you and you are upset, isn't that it?"

"Mother!"

Flame cast herself down again into the pillows and began to sob despairingly. But what was the good . . . what sympathy would she get here? Other girls had mothers that they could turn to.

"Mother, I have an awful terror that because someone kissed me desperately hard I might have a baby . . . do tell me that I couldn't."

How easy it would be to say to some mothers. But to hers? Impossible! Besides, there was always the awful fear that she would hear her own terror confirmed.

No, better not to know; better just to marry this awful man, and get away from home and chance about the baby, and have Nigel and his friends to stay and make the best of it.

"Stop crying, Flame. You will make a perfect object of yourself." Lady Peterson's voice came cold as ice over the eiderdown.

"Mother, if only you . . ." Flame's disfigured face reappeared, pathetic in its despair.

"If only I what? Don't be ridiculous and hysterical, Flame. Tell me quietly what has happened."

"If only you would wait just a minute till I have washed my face, I will tell you everything that has happened," returned Flame evenly.

She swung her legs over the side of the bed preparatory to getting off it.

For her self-control had come back with a rush. Humiliate herself before this mother of ice and snow! Never!

She sponged and powdered, and finally ran the silver-backed comb through her hair with a gentle self-possession that gave very little indication of the storm that had just passed.

"Well?" But there was eagerness beneath the cold interrogative.

"Well, Lord Lovegrove did ask me to marry him," she said.

In spite of her desperate efforts to control her voice it did tremble a little as she continued.

"But I did not give him any answer. In fact, I didn't wait to give him any answer, I dashed straight away up here and lay down on the bed."

"And why did you do that?"

"Because I was excited," lied Flame steadfastly.

"It was unwise," said Lady Peterson slowly. "Lord Lovegrove is a very excellent match and he may be offended. There is always the chance that he may not renew his offer."

"I think he will, if I go anywhere near him," said Flame with horrible intuition.

"Well, then, the best thing that you can do is to go back into the garden at once and find him," said Lady Peterson, getting up instantly.

"What, now?" cried out Flame, off her guard.

"Yes, of course now." Lady Peterson's downbent eyes were like frozen wells. "Don't tell me, Flame, that you are contemplating anything so wildly foolish as a refusal."

"Mother, I don't think I really love him."

This, in spite of Flame's desperate efforts not to say it, burst from her.

Lady Peterson smiled a little, and the smile was a very cruel one.

"Love!" she said. "We are not talking about love, Flame, that comes afterwards. We are now discussing marriage, and a very excellent one, too."

"But if you marry a person it is for ever," stuttered Flame, holding two trembling hands cupped over a bluish flicker.

"Not of necessity," said Lady Peterson, staring out of the window, and remembering her dead husband.

"It generally is," said Flame despairingly.

Lady Peterson withdrew her eyes from the window and levelled them on the child in front of her.

"Why is your mouth all smudged and turning blue in one place?"

"Mother, he kissed me so hard," said Flame, all her being suddenly one great despairing outcry.

Now she would hear it, her death sentence!

"Then of course you must marry him," said Lady Peterson decidedly.

She half got up out of the flowered chair.

"Why must I?" asked Flame, now reckless with despair.

After all, why not hear it?

"Beause no decent girl allows a man to kiss her, as Lord Lovegrove has evidently kissed you, without marrying him," said Lady Peterson decidedly.

She started to walk towards the door.

Flame followed her across the carpet, a tragic

little figure with outstretched hands, pleading for a little sympathy from this mother of stone.

"Mother, do wait a minute, I want to ask you something else," she cried.

But Lady Peterson had a sort of dim, shadowy idea of what Flame was going to say. With deliberate brutality she struck back the question on to the trembling lips.

After all, as she thought, one well-manicured hand on the glass door-knob, already her lover had begun to criticize her, and that on account of this child of hers. She turned round.

"Flame," she said, "don't ask me any questions the answer to which you will be very sorry to hear. I have said enough. Go out into the garden again, and tell Lord Lovegrove that you will be proud and glad to be his wife."

Lady Peterson opened the door and shut it behind her.

Flame stood stock-still in the middle of the floor. Then it was true what she had thought. What else could her mother mean by saying "the answer to which you will be very sorry to hear"?

Dreadful enveloping, spreading kisses like she had had in the garden brought a baby in some mysterious way.

Flame shrank and froze.

She stood, head hanging, hands clenched by her sides, until the quiet closing of a door farther along the corridor showed that her mother was back in her own bedroom.

With a small hand that slipped and stuck she twisted the big glass knob of her own door.

Slowly she went back to the garden. Very reluctantly she agreed to marry Lord Lovegrove.

Chapter
Two

Colonel Forsythe did not see Flame for about six weeks after her engagement.

He had been sent for rather hurriedly by the doctor in charge of the sanatorium in Switzerland, where his wife lay out on a balcony gazing with slowly dying eyes at the heavenly glory of the Alps spread out in front of her.

"Gerald, I am so happy," she said.

She turned her eyes from the snows to let them rest on the burly figure in Harris tweed by her side.

"Are you, darling?" said Colonel Forsythe.

To his credit he spent almost the whole of his not very large income in ensuring that his wife's last days on this earth should be made as happy and comfortable as possible.

"Yes, I am, except just for one thing," replied Mrs Forsythe.

"Tell me, then, dear," he said.

He crossed one thick burly leg over the other.

"Well, it's this," replied Mrs Forsythe, and her transparent face flushed. "I know you will want to marry again, Gerald, and I wish you to. But I do not want you to marry Lady Peterson, she is a hard and unscrupulous woman, and she will end by making you terribly unhappy."

Colonel Forsythe also flushed, and he shifted his position rather uncomfortably.

"Oh, don't worry about that, dear."

"I don't exactly worry, because I seem to have lost that art," said Mrs Forsythe gently, "besides, when it is only a step out of this world into the next, it would be foolish to waste one's time in worrying."

She looked with worried eyes and went on.

"Promise me, dear, that you would not marry Lady Peterson and I should go very much more happily."

"Come, come, Agnes, it's hardly fair to tie me down."

Desperately uncomfortable and miserable, Colonel Forsythe got up and began to pace about the glazed verandah.

"It is for your own happiness, dear," said Mrs Forsythe.

Her pale eyes followed the burly figure in its agitated pacing.

Later that night he was called to his dying wife's side and he gave her his promise.

So it was quite six weeks before Colonel Forsythe went down to Falaise again. But when he saw Flame he was horrified, and he said so to the woman who followed him round with the eyes of a whipped spaniel.

"That child will die, if you don't take care," he said one night when Flame came in to say good night after an evening spent with her lover in the billiard-room.

"Die! Rubbish, Gerald, you are getting foolish in your old age."

"How you can allow the child to be shut up for hours with the old beast, I can't conceive," went on Colonel Forsythe angrily.

Lady Peterson flushed with anger, but she knew better than to show she was angry. She did not belong legally to this man yet. Until she did she would have to be careful.

"Flame is going to be married in a little over three weeks," she said smoothly, "and until she is, she is sure to look odd and unstrung. Girls always do when they are engaged, and Flame is young for her age."

"The whole thing's preposterous!" burst out Colonel Forsythe.

Flame's wan and bleached little face had made a very disquieting impression on him.

Lovegrove was a satyr, and it was murder to throw the child to him. He got up and began to walk about the room. Lady Peterson watched him, and in her heart that most deadly of all poisons began to work, the jealousy of a mother of her child.

Flame was young and beautiful, and this middle-aged man whom she worshipped had found it out.

She must be got rid of, somehow. Another three weeks! And anything might happen in three weeks. . . . Flame must go away and not come back until immediately before her wedding-day.

A couple of days in town would complete the trousseau shopping. She spoke quietly.

"Don't worry, Gerald," she said. "After all, I understand Flame very well, and I felt very much as she does during my own engagement."

The corridors at Falaise were long and echoing and very still, when Colonel Forsythe opened his heavy oak door. He listened carefully and glanced swiftly up and down once or twice.

He walked slowly, thinking deeply, his clean-shaven chin dropped on his bare throat.

This affair would have to come to an end ... but he would let Flame's wedding get over first. She would make such a hell of a row if he smashed it all up suddenly.

He would plead an unexpected call aboard ... big-game shooting, anything, and then, once away, he could write. After all, she had really brought it on herself.

You can't stand by and see a pretty child sacrificed and then take the executioner to your heart!

Outside Flame's door he stopped, moved by a sudden feeling of compassion. She was such a child, he might easily have been her father. There she was, so bitterly alone at a time like this, when a girl wanted her mother.

Gad! If he had been her father, wouldn't that lascivious old beast downstairs have had the order of the boot! Colonel Forsythe drew a long breath and very nearly turned to go back to his own room.

Then he heard a sound of sobs torn up from the depth of a heart very near to breaking point. Colonel Forsythe, moved by an impulse for which afterwards he thanked God, opened Flame's door and went in.

At first he could not see anything.

Then he did, guided by a shaft of moonlight that came stealing through the softly blowing muslin curtains.

Flame was kneeling upon the bed in the corner, her yellow head buried in her hands.

The piteous sobs came strangling up from the depth of her; for some reason or other this child found herself in hell.

Colonel Forsythe came to the abrupt conclusion that it was his business to find out why.

He came quietly across the carpet, his hands still in his pockets.

But Flame heard him come, and the sobs ceased instantly.

There was a palpitating silence of intensest terror.

"Who is it?" she asked.

"It's only me."

Colonel Forsythe hardly knew what shyness was, but there was something in the little figure kneeling upon the bed in the scanty nightdress and the virginal whiteness of the whole room that affected him oddly.

"What's the matter?"

Colonel Forsythe had reached the side of the bed and was holding out a kind hand.

"How did you know I wasn't in bed?"

"I was passing, and I heard you crying. Tell me what's wrong, Flame. It isn't right that you should cry like this. Tell me."

Colonel Forsythe sat down on the edge of the bed.

"I only cry because I am tired." Flame's spirit was instantly on guard.

"No, you don't. Little girls don't get as tired as all that. You're unhappy about something. Tell me, dear, and I may be able to help you."

Flame suddenly crouched lower.

"You'll tell Mother," she said.

The sobs began again.

"I shall not do anything of the kind. Come, come!"

Colonel Forsythe put out a firm hand and took hold of Flame's arm.

"Come along on to my knee and tell me all about it," he said.

He bundled her up in the eiderdown, and carried her to a big wicker chair seen vaguely outlined against the window.

"Gerald, Gerald! . . ."

The comfort of the kind touch of human arms in this hour of her extremity was too much for Flame, and she burrowed her head into the striped silk shoulder and cried until she could cry no more.

Colonel Forsythe took hold of the little pointed chin.

"Enough, all this salt will take out the colour of my stripes, and Johnson will give me socks for spoiling my new pyjamas. Now, then, what's it all about, Flame? Make a clean breast of it."

Out it all came. Colonel Forsythe, listening, snapped his bull-dog jaws once or twice and ground his teeth. And then he spoke, and there was mystification in his voice:

"But why in the name of goodness have you gone on with the thing so long?" he said. "You don't like the man; well, then you must break with him. No one can force you into a marriage that is utterly repugnant to you, Flame."

After a silence of extreme anguish, Flame spoke.

Colonel Forsythe, seeing the little face shriveled in the pale moonlight, knew with an awful certainty what he was going to hear.

"I must marry him," she said; "I am going to have a baby."

Colonel Forsythe let her slip gently off his knees. He felt he must stand up and walk about, or something would go "phut" in his head. That scented, padded, lecherous brute in the corridor down below!

God, he would beat out his brains on those polished boards before he was many hours older, beat them out slowly, a blow for each hour of misery that he had caused this child.

Have a baby! This girl not much more than a baby herself! Ah-h-h-! And there was vengeance unspeakable in that low, drawn-out exclamation.

"Gerald, you're beginning to loathe me!"

Flame made a little passionate run to the side of the pacing figure, and caught hold of the striped coat.

"No, I'm not!" Colonel Forsythe's response was instant.

He caught the little hands to his broad chest and held them there.

"It's not that, dear, don't think it for a moment. It's only that . . ."

Colonel Forsythe's voice failed him, and the dark blood surged up into his forehead, and receded, leaving it wet.

"Tell me about it if you can, dear," he said gently.

"Oh, I will, I will! Let me sit down on your knee again, and I will tell you everything," she said.

She began to drag him, like a child, towards the big chair.

Gerald Forsythe sat down. Very slowly Flame

told him of the passionate kisses Lord Lovegrove had forced on her.

Colonel Forsythe began to see light a little, and his first sensation, after the one of stupefying blinding relief, was one of fiercest, bitterest disgust and anger with this child's mother.

Any woman ought to have known, or any rate have had the sense to find out, what was at the bottom of Flame's obvious and constant misery. Gad! Agnes had been right; he would clear out of it the very next day. . . .

"Look here, dear," he said.

His voice was so kind that Flame clung to him anew, wondering in the depths of her gentle little heart why Nigel had always been so hard on Colonel Forsythe.

"Look here, dear, it's rather difficult to explain. But if you're hanging on to your engagement because you think you're going to have a baby, you need not do it anymore. You're not, there isn't the remotest, vaguest chance of it."

"Gerald, how do you know?" she said.

"How do I know?"

Colonel Forsythe laughed low down in his throat, a laugh that made even Flame, shaken as she was, want to laugh too, it sounded so very amused.

"How do I know? Well, I know because I am a very old man compared to you, Flame, and I have seen a good deal of the ways of the world."

"But doesn't spreedy kissing bring a baby, then?" asked Flame.

She was still feeling uncertain and stupid, and longing to hear the words of reprieve again and again.

"No, thank Heaven!" said Colonel Forsythe. "Flame, don't be such a goose. Ask your mother about these things; she is the proper person to tell you."

"Mother!"

There was a world of scorn in the young voice. "Mother! Gerald, how could I?"

Flame got resolutely off the muscular knee.

"No, I would far rather ask Waterton anything like that, or Nigel. But there is nothing to ask anyone now, because I know. God has delivered me."

Flame's voice was solemn.

"Now all I have to do is to tell Lord Lovegrove that I have made a mistake, and then settle down again in peace."

Colonel Forsythe was standing up, very square and burly in his striped pyjamas, but his rather underhung jaw was set in an anxious line.

This wasn't going to be as easy as Flame thought it was, and he tried to say so, as gently and reassuringly as he could.

But Flame was calm.

"I shall manage it all right. Nigel and I together can generally do things."

But Colonel Forsythe had been right when he said to Flame that he did not think that things would go as easily as she imagined.

Lady Peterson was white with rage at this sudden collapse of her plans, and decided at once to send her away to a convent.

When Flame heard of this she immediately cabled Nigel.

He arrived the next day and found out from Waterton exactly what had happened. He said the only solution would be for Flame to disguise herself as a boy and run away to India where he knew Waterton had some relations.

Flame was quite excited at the idea although horrified that people would find out she was really a girl.

"Supposing I were ill?" said Flame. "People might come poking about and find out."

"Don't make objections, Flame." Nigel spoke rather impatiently.

"You speak as if it were all settled," said Flame wonderingly.

She stared across the big white bearskin hearth-rug.

"It is," said Nigel firmly. "Waterton and I fixed it all up before you came in this evening."

"Nigel, but what shall I do when I get to Bombay?"

Flame was gasping at this sudden smashing dislocation of the whole of her life. Go out to India dressed as a boy . . . the very thought was convulsing.

"Nigel, who's going to pay?" she gasped.

"Waterton, he's rather well off, so he says."

But at this Nigel did falter a little. That was the one blot on the wonderful plan, that he had had to depend on the old servant for the where-withal to carry it out.

"Nigel, but it seems so awful!" Flame's lower lip was trembling.

"How awful?" demanded Nigel. "Wouldn't it be more awful to either marry that old horror or be a nun?"

"Yes, but Mother might get me back some-how. Or someone might see by my shape that I wasn't really a boy," faltered Flame.

She let her crimsoning glance fall into her lap.

"You haven't any shape to speak of," said her brother frankly, "at least, none that you can't manage by pulling out your skirt a bit. And as to Mother getting you back, how can she, Flame, if you are in the middle of the sea?

"Now, I ask you, don't you think you really are being rather tiresome and futile?

"Pull yourself together a bit. Waterton and I are helping you to escape from a most ghastly fate, and all you can do is to find fault with the plans we make. It's pretty discouraging, to put it mildly."

"I don't mean to be discouraging," Flame was faltering and tearful, "and I am truly, truly grateful, Nigel."

Flame got up and came across the hearthrug with outstretched hands.

"But it's only that, when you haven't been about very much, to hear that you've suddenly got to start off for anywhere as far as India, dressed up as a boy, does seem rather terrifying."

Nigel was ruffling the yellow hair with a derisive but affectionate hand.

"Once you're started, you'll love it. Think of tomorrow, Flame; London! Lunch at a restaurant, rushing round for passages and passports. We'll have the time of our lives."

"Oh, yes, that will be heavenly!"

Flame lifted her head, restored.

London with Nigel would be bliss.

She had hardly ever been to London, only for dull things like the dentist, and then always with either her mother or her governess.

"I begin to feel that it may be fun," she said, and smiled widely.

"Good for you!" returned her brother, more relieved than he liked to express.

Because nobody took much notice of the two youths when they arrived in London, it did not take Nigel long to get Flame rigged out for the journey.

Getting a passport was going to be more difficult, and take some time. Nigel told Flame to wait for him in Westminster Abbey.

"Kindly remove your hat, sir."

A black-gowned figure with terribly menacing eyes was at her elbow, when she entered the abbey, an angry custodian, looking like a bat in his black gown, frowning heavily.

"Oh, yes, of course."

Flame dragged in a panic at the bowler and held it down close to her side. Not safe yet. Yes, the custodian had turned away, bending an attentive ear to a whispering clergyman.

Flame walked down the aisle behind a little trail of what looked like a mother's meeting out for a treat. She would sit down somewhere, kneel down somewhere. . . .

The minutes on her knees in the dark shadow of one of the monuments restored Flame's equilibrium. She could think again . . . breathe again.

The abbey was filling up, people coming in from different parts of it, and all walking past where she sat, up more towards the front. There must be a service. Joy! she would come in for it.

Flame got up and walked further towards the front too.

"Are we allowed to sit there?"

With enormous courage, Flame had accosted one of the bats. Fortunately this particular bat had sons of its own, so it smiled back into the clear grey eyes.

"Yes, sir," he said, and unhooked the big twisted red rope to let Flame pass into the chancel.

"Lord, it's too beautiful!" Flame, imaginative and musical to her very soul, was gripping her hands between her knees in a wild effort for self-control.

What did it make her feel like, this?

It made her feel as if she wanted to gather her soul up in two hands and hold it out as an offering to someone, as if she wanted to sob out all her joys and fears at somebody's feet, to give herself in a wild surrender of body, soul, and spirit.

Flame stared out into the blurred gloom, her face white and tense.

Hugh Keymer, sitting opposite, leaning back with long legs crossed, watched her, and thought what a desperate pity it was that a boy with a face like that had ever to grow up.

It was like seeing something very beautiful, like a piece of Venetian glass, and knowing that it was going to be smashed in a couple of hours.

He sighed and turned away. Flame's eyes had met his.

The vibrating, burring stop of the great organ had ceased.

This must be a Lesson . . . Flame sat back, but she still stared at the man in the stall opposite to her.

There was something about his face that made you want to stare.

What was it?

There was plenty of time to find out, because the Lesson was a very long one.

So she gave herself up to the contemplation of the face that showed palely against the black carved background of the stall.

It was not quite a young face; it had too many lines on it, and also the hair was sprinkled with grey. But it was the mouth that enchanted Flame most.

It was set in lines of heavenly kindness, kindness and endurance. Flame came to the conclusion that those were the two things about it that made her want to look at it so much.

It was as if the person had realized that everything was all wrong and hopeless for him, but that he was going, because of that, to try and make it nicer for other people.

He would be a heavenly person to tell things to, because he would so absolutely understand. . . .

As Flame thought this, the sound of the organ crept through the arches and aisles again, and Flame was lost in the *Magnificat*.

She did not notice the man again until the very end, when they were all standing to let the choir pass out.

He was very tall and broad, and he had an extremely nice tie on and a striped grey flannel suit.

She slipped out of her seat so that she should walk out behind him; she wanted to see his hands. Hands meant such a lot; you could tell by hands and mouth what a person was really like.

Flame had the unerring instinct of extreme youth.

His hands were as nice as the rest of him.

Flame saw that before he forged a little ahead and was lost in the crowd.

Nigel met Flame outside Westminster Abbey and told her he had everything arranged.

"Now we'll get a taxi and pick up our luggage at Waterloo. Then we'll book in at the Strand Palace Hotel. It's always crammed, so we shan't be seen. I'd rather go to the Rubens, but I daren't. But the money I've spent!"

Nigel groaned as he scrutinized the absurdly modest bill.

"Have you got enough to pay for the hotel?"

"Of course I have, silly, and enough to give you about twenty pounds to take with you. But that doesn't mean that I haven't spent a large amount of money, because I have."

"Oh, well, as long as you've got some left it's all right."

Flame had begun to enjoy herself again.

She was also beginning to love the feeling of being able to kick her legs about. She got into the taxi with a feeling of wild adventure and exhilaration.

Waterloo did not take long, nor did the interview at the office in the hall of the Strand Palace Hotel. Brother and sister found themselves being whisked upwards in a lift that made a sweet, soft noise like a kettle boiling.

"Oh, heavenly! There's a door in between our rooms."

Flame stood in the middle of the carpet flapping her coat up and down. This was real excitement, a hotel all by themselves. And down below them the sonorous roar of London. She laughed jubilantly.

"Don't get excited!"

But Nigel was also enjoying himself enormously. It was such a relief to feel themselves under a roof with everything done. Now there was really nothing to do until the next day, when he saw Flame off at Liverpool Street.

But to do nothing for a whole evening, with all its glorious possibilities!

It was too tantalizing.

Besides, it would give Flame a chance to get into evening clothes. No, they would go out and enjoy themselves and chance being seen.

"Look here, we'll go to a theatre," he said abruptly.

"Nigel, by ourselves!" Flame said breathlessly.

"Yes, of course. You unpack and if you can't manage anything, give me a shout."

"What?" Shall I have to put on evening clothes?"

"Of course. Go and have a bath; you need it, your face is absolutely black. It's at the end of the corridor. Put on your bathgown, and hurry up."

Nigel chose *The Girl in the Jam Puff*, but he rather regretted his choice. Flame, who had never been to anything more than a pantomime, was in convulsions of laughter from beginning to end.

"Don't make such a row!" Nigel was also laughing, only more reluctantly.

Flame was beginning to make them conspicuous. It alarmed him. "Don't make such a row or I shall take you out."

"Not before it's finished?" Flame said petrified.

"Yes, I shall if you make a row so that people turn round. Shut up and enjoy it quietly. Your tie's all under one ear too. You are hopeless. Pull it back."

"Which way?"

Flame was hauling wildly, her small face grave again. Nigel was going to get cross; now everything would be spoilt.

"The other way."

Nigel cast an uneasy glance sideways. Flame did not look in the least like a boy now. She had a sort of wild look on her face that a boy never got, and her hair was all rough.

"Away from me!" he hissed.

"Is that right?"

By now Flame could easily have cried, and her hands were damp and nervous.

"Better."

Nigel riveted his attention on the stage again, and Flame tried to follow suit.

But she was shaken and a little unhappy. When the heavy plush curtains fell together after the last act but one, she tugged at her brother's sleeve.

"I want to go out," she whispered.

"Why?" Nigel had begun to enjoy himself again; besides, it was not safe to go out with the lights up.

"You're cross and it makes me miserable. Besides, look over there; it's Gerald in that box. Supposing he sees us, he will tell Mother."

"Gerald! Where?"

"There, with that lady with hardly any back to her dress. Nigel, are you allowed to dress like that in public?"

"Keep your head down." Nigel was hissing with terror.

Oh, for the lights to go out again! They were

done if Colonel Forsythe saw them, and people had a ghastly way of looking at you if you were thinking or talking about them.

There! he had turned, and was looking their way. Now he had leaned forward and picked up the opera-glasses from the velvet ledge.

"Keep your head down."

Nigel, with his own chin on his shirt-front, was white with fear.

"Seen a ghost, Gerry?"

The lady with Colonel Forsythe was looking at him rather curiously. What was he staring at all of a sudden? she wondered. She settled her skirt a little resentfully.

But Colonel Forsythe did not answer; he was out of the box and halfway down the red carpeted stairs before she had realized he was gone.

"He's gone," Flame, who had been peeping up under her long lashes, whispered excitedly.

"Gone where? Oh, thank God!" for the orchestra had struck up again, and the lights had gone out with a wink. "Flame, we must clear out of this at once. Don't wait for anything; just follow me."

"Before the end?"

But Nigel silenced any protest by a sharp backward kick, and Flame followed her brother without any further demur. But they were too late.

Gerald Forsythe was standing waiting for them in the red and gold circular foyer. He was lighting a cigarette.

"Hallo, Nigel!" He only glanced casually at the second figure in evening dress. "Where are you staying?"

"At the Strand Palace."

Nigel Peterson's mouth was shaking in spite of his desperate efforts to control it.

"Well, I'll be round by half-past eleven; don't go to bed, will you?"

"No, all right."

But Nigel swung round with despair in his heart. He felt he had been an utter fool not to have stayed home for that evening.

"Come on." He spoke roughly over his shoulder to his sister.

"Well?" Colonel Forsythe had his sturdy legs crossed.

The lift, with its singing noise of nearly boiling water, had just deposited him on the third floor of the Strand Palace Hotel.

"Well, you've done us down, that's all."

If Nigel had done what he wanted to do, he would have cast himself down on the bed and shed bitter tears.

"Well, but what does it mean?" Colonel Forsythe nodded towards the second door.

"Is Flame in there?"

"Yes."

"Well, carry on, I want to hear."

"There's nothing to tell you—it's obvious. You know as much as I do about Flame's engagement having been broken off. Well, according to Flame and Waterton, Mother's all out to get her into a convent in France.

"Flame wired to me in an awful flap, and I got leave from the Head and came up. The rest you see. I dressed her up in my clothes and to-morrow she was to have sailed for Bombay."

"Bombay?"

"Yes, Waterton's got a married daughter out there."

"But what in Heaven's name! . . ."

"Oh, shut up, you don't know Mother as I do!"

Then a tear did find its way out from under the faintly freckled eyelid, and Nigel flung himself down in a chair.

Flame! Her life would be hell from this time forward, and he would be able to do nothing.

Colonel Forsythe sat a little forward, moved, in spite of himself. It was a harebrained scheme, to give it its mildest term.

But he had had a prolonged scene that afternoon with this boy's mother at the Grosvenor Hotel, and the memory of it still lingered.

"Look here," he said.

The communicating door opened and Flame came in.

"Clear out, Flame!" Nigel jerked up an angry head.

"No, don't, because Gerald will do as I ask him, because he's already been most kind to me. Gerald . . ."

Flame, looking delicious in the short black dinner-jacket, fell on her knees beside the big chair.

"Gerald, you were kind to me before, when I easily could have died with misery; be kind now and don't upset our plans. Nigel's got the ticket and everything, and I don't know what he hasn't spent. Don't upset it, darling, darling, Gerald."

"Shut up, Flame."

But Colonel Forsythe interrupted, laying a

gentle hand on the bowed yellow head. She might have been his own daughter.

The woman certainly had the temper of a fiend.

"Leave her alone, Nigel, she's right in a way. I don't want to butt in, but I must know this: has Flame anywhere certain to go to at the other end? If not, I must put a stopper on it."

"Oh, I have, I have!" Flame broke in excitedly. "I know Waterton's married daughter; she often used to come and have tea with us in the nursery."

"And . . ." Colonel Forsythe broke off and glanced across the room. "I'll settle it all with Nigel, you go to bed, Flame. But I promise you this, that unless when we have talked it all out there seems any very violent reason why you shouldn't go, I won't interfere.

"But you must promise me this, Flame, that you will write to me from every port and tell me how you are getting on."

Colonel Forsythe beamed contentedly. After all, he thought, as Flame after a grateful kiss closed the door behind her, what was it to do with him?

He had broken with their mother, and there his responsibility ended. Left alone to the tender mercies of that termagant, what might not become of that gentle little child?

He turned again to the boy in front of him.

But later, as he crossed Trafalgar Square, he did have one or two very severe twinges of conscience. A man of his age, dealing with two children like that, ought to have immediately telephoned to the Grosvenor and had them handed over into the charge of their mother.

Then he shook his head as he visualized the mother as he had last seen her. No, no, anything but that. And that nice boy . . . how thankful he was that he had cut clear of the whole thing.

It hadn't been right to let it go on so long, it hadn't been right.

Chapter
Three

Liverpool Street Station is not an inspiring spot to be seen off from. Flame, clutching her umbrella-case and Burberry, thought it the most dreary station she had ever been in.

"Nigel ... I can't!" She suddenly burst out crying.

"You must, it's the only thing now. Don't cry, dear." Nigel's young face was rigid. "Here, hop into this 'first'; there's no one in it."

He laid the coat and umbrella down on the padded seat.

"Flame, darling old thing, darling old girl, good-bye ..."

Nigel Peterson made a great sobbing choke in his throat as he clutched his sister.

"Nigel, supposing anything happens to you while I'm away ... supposing you die?"

The slim figure in the lounge suit was rent with sobs. Oh, the awful, awful misery of all this! Wouldn't it have been better to marry Lord Love-grove after all? Then she would at least have been able to have Nigel to stay.

"Oh, Nigel, must I go . . . must I go?"

"Yes, of course you must."

Flame's collapse steadied her brother.

"Of course you must, and you'll love it when you're once started. It's only the beginning that's so miserable. Here, wipe your eyes, Flame, some-one's coming and they'll see."

"Not in here?"

"Yes, I expect they are, you can't keep it to yourself. Now then, I won't hang about anymore, give me a good hug and then I'll go."

With one more convulsive squeeze Nigel Peterson was gone, diving through the groups of people gathered in little knots on the platform, the tears running unchecked down his cheeks.

Left alone, Flame sank down in the corner of the compartment and gave way to unrestrained tears.

Nigel had gone, Nigel, the one person in the world, except Waterton, that she loved.

Here she was, absolutely alone with this des-perate journey in front of her.

Then, to her horror, there were voices out-side the carriage and the handle was twisted round, and a woman stepped up into the compartment, a despatch-case in her hand.

"Yes, I'll have all the small things in here, please. Doris, don't you wait."

There were tears in the eyes and voice of the woman speaking. Flame, who up to that moment had been rather interested, buried her face in her handkerchief and wept anew.

Embarking on a big liner is a very bewilder-ing thing, especially if you are new to it. Flame lurched along up the slanting gangway with a stream of other people.

Nobody paid the slightest attention to her; they were all far too much absorbed in their own affairs. "First Saloon to the right, please." Flame was headed off in her efforts to enter the second class by a kindly man in white uniform.

She stumbled along a passage smelling of paint, an enormously long passage with low curtained doors on both sides of it. What was this? Did they sleep in those funny little boxes then?

Flame, suddenly curious, thrust her head into one.

"What do you want? This is a ladies' cabin."

It was an elderly lady who spoke, very angrily, and Flame backed out again in a panic. How awful to be shut up with someone like that for three weeks! How thankful she was that she had a cabin to herself!

Ninety pounds, you would be sure to get the very best for that. She wandered on, beginning to enjoy the novelty of it all.

"Hallo! So you've got on safely."

It was Dr Lane, who had travelled down with her.

"I lost you when I came out from the doctor."

"Yes, but somebody pushed me the way I had to go." Flame smiled broadly.

How grown-up this all made her feel.

"I'm looking for my cabin."

"I expect you're on the Hurricane Deck; most of the men are. We poor females have to be content with deck cabins," Dr Lane sighed with a smile.

"The Hurricane Deck!"

Flame, smiling to herself, went on.

It sounded lovely and breezy, how she hoped that her cabin would be up there. Twenty-eight her number was; Nigel had written it on her labels.

"Can you tell me where cabin number twenty-eight is, please?" she said.

She had come to the end of the corridor, and was in a huge saloon full of long tables, beautifully laid for a meal. She spoke to an English steward.

"You'll find that on the Hurricane Deck, sir. Up the stairs and out to the right."

"Oh, thank you!"

Flame went on again, this time enormously intrigued. Like a child diverted, her misery had gone for the moment.

She walked along a little, breathing in the cool air. This looked like cabins. Yes, here was hers, numbers twenty-seven, twenty-eight.

She pushed aside the heavy curtain and went in. It was a nice cabin, very large, with a port-hole that gave on to the deck. There were two berths, spotlessly white and neat, one on each side of the bluey carpet.

Each berth was covered with luggage!

"How can there be two people?"

Flame's breath suddenly caught in her throat.

What did it mean, what did it mean? Nigel had said a cabin to herself, had he or hadn't he? Anyhow, of course it must be like that. How could she . . . ?

She fled to the door and stared at the little label, so neat in its brass rim: "No. 27 Mr Hugh Keymer"; "No. 28 Mr Nigel Peterson." Flame fled back again, and dragging the curtain across the brass rod behind her, she crouched down on her suitcase, holding her clenched hands over her ears.

What should she do, what should she do? It must be changed. . . . She would find the woman who had come down in the train with her and ask her. She got up and fled down the stairs again.

"What do you do if you don't like the sound of the person who's in your cabin?"

Flame had dashed along the passage and flung herself through the crimson serge curtain where she could hear Dr Lane talking.

"Will you kindly go outside, please?"

It was Dr Lane's friend who was speaking, furiously angry, with her hair streaming down her back in two pigtails.

"What on earth is the matter?"

Dr Lane began to laugh. Was the boy deficient in some way? she wondered with professional curiosity.

"You mustn't dash into women's cabins like this, you know," she said, pushing Flame gently backwards. "Go outside, and I'll come out."

"Go to the purser if you really want anything altered," she said, when she had heard Flame to a tumultuous end. "Although I happen to know Mr Keymer, and I am sure you would find him a very kind and considerate cabin-companion. However, if you are set on it . . . But I warn you that you will find it a very difficult thing to get it altered."

But Flame was already halfway down the corridor.

Dr Lane watched her go and then turned back into her own cabin. There was something funny about that boy; she would keep her eye on him.

The purser, already harassed to death, wasted very little time on the distracted boy with staring eyes.

"Altered, of course not! Cabin to yourself, rubbish! We're packed like sardines as it is. Yes, come in, Ferguson . . ."

As there was not room for three people in the cabin at once, Flame had to beat a retreat before a burly ship's officer.

"Lord, what shall I do?"

Flame was tearing up the stairs again. She would at any rate put all the other person's luggage outside.

She fled by the two men leaning against the wall at the end of the little corridor and began feverishly to collect it. The rugs first. . . .

"I say, leave my things alone, please."

One of the men leaning against the wall had turned and was staring.

"What damned cheek!" he remarked to his friend. "I'd better get along in before the kid bags all the pegs. Yes, see you later. . . ."

Hugh Keymer came lounging along the corridor and stood in the narrow door, entirely filling it up.

"I say, my young friend, don't be so free with other people's belongings. This is your first voyage, I gather, but it's my fifth, so I'll settle how things are done in this cabin. To begin with, we can't both unpack at once, so you clear out until I've finished."

"I can't share a cabin with anyone else," Flame answered in a trembling voice.

"I am afraid that does not concern me," Hugh Keymer replied, stooping over a suit-case preparatory to unfastening its straps. "Get out of the way, please."

Flame slunk out, shivering with misery and fear. This was more ghastly than anything she had ever imagined.

What should she do?

Get off, while there was yet time. The thought went through her head like lightning. Nigel would understand that she couldn't dress and undress with a strange man in the room.

She dashed down the companion stairs.

Back at the open hatch through which she had come in the first instance she was pulled up short. A slowly widening strip of greenish water lay between her and the landing-stage.

A powerful sailor laid a none-too-gentle hand on her shoulder. "Stand back there, sir, please," he said: "the passengers are not allowed down below now. Upstairs on the left for the saloon deck."

"I want to get off," Flame sobbed.

"I'm afraid you've left it too late, sonnie," the sailor answered, smiling absently, his big hand cupped for a shout to the crowd in a state of feverish activity on the quay.

"Let go there!" he bellowed, not taking any more notice of Flame.

Nothing remains acutely awful for very long, especially to the very young.

By the time Flame had stopped crying, and had watched the people a little, and had felt a few pangs of very healthy hunger, she felt very much better.

When a bugle rang out, and gloomy people

turned from their staring at the river down which
they were majestically proceeding, and started
off for somewhere else, she followed them, her
small hands stuck jauntily in her pockets.

Flame sat next to a motherly-looking lady
called Mrs Holroyd-Browne, who helped her get
through her lunch and explain all the different
things.

When, after a good deal of fruit salad and
cream and a cup of excellent coffee, she slid out
of her revolving chair, she felt that she really was
going to enjoy herself enormously.

"And what are you going to do now?" said
Mrs Holroyd-Browne.

She had caught Flame up at the foot of the
stairs.

"Have you got a deck chair?"

"No, I haven't," said Flame blankly. "I
didn't know I should want one."

"Of course you will." Mrs Holroyd-Browne
laughed musically. You must hire one from the
deck steward; it's quite simple. Only get hold
of him soon, before all the best ones are
gone."

So Flame went off in search of the deck
steward, and the chair was produced, and set down
next to Mrs Holroyd-Browne's in a delightfully
sheltered corner.

But before she sat down Flame spied a tall
figure in the distance. That was her cabin companion, and it meant that the cabin was clear for
her to unpack.

She must go at once.

"I say, I've got to go and unpack," she said.

"Not at once, surely," said Mrs Holroyd-
Browne reproachfully.

"Yes, now, this instant, or I may not get an-other chance," Flame replied.

Her small feet twinkled over the spotless boards of the deck.

Mr Keymer was a very neat man; Flame came to that conclusion swiftly. Everything in the cabin was so neatly arranged.

It did not take long to unpack, Flame was travelling light, and it did not take long either to fill the two empty drawers with the clothes she possessed.

She looked with pleasure on the four pairs of white flannel trousers and blue blazer. She would wear some of those tomorrow, she decided. She laid her evening suit carefully away.

What a mercy she had had a chance of trying it on. Now she would be able to manage it all right; otherwise the collar might have stumped her.

"Getting on all right?"

Hugh Keymer had been rather regretting his brusque treatment of the boy who shared his cab-in. He had sat next to Dr Lane at lunch, and she had told him how he had cried all the way down to Tilbury.

So he thought he would stroll along to the cabin and have a look at him.

"Oh yes, thank you," said Flame, looking up with a bright smile.

This man had a nice face, after all, a *good* face.

"Hallo! You're the man I saw in Westminster Abbey," she exclaimed after an astounded pause.

"Westminster Abbey!" Hugh Keymer was mystified.

Then he remembered, and smiled. "Of course. I thought I had seen you somewhere before. You sat opposite me in the chancel."

"Yes, I did," said Flame. "Oh, wasn't it heavenly?"

She sat down abruptly on the edge of her berth. "Do you know, I've never felt that sort of singing feeling in my *soul* before. As if you wanted to drag out all the feeling part of you, and cast it down at somebody's feet."

"My sainted aunt!"

Hugh Keymer spoke *sotto voce* and with conscious discomfort.

Was the boy dotty, as Hester had rather implied? If so, he was in for a cheerful voyage!

"No, I don't know the feeling, I am glad to say," he replied rather frigidly; "anyhow, I just came along to see that you were all right; take the pegs that are left."

Hugh Keymer, his hands thrust deep into his pockets, went out again.

Flame, left alone, sighed.

"He seems a little touchy," she said.

She got her sponge out of its waterproof bag, with her feelings down at zero again.

Three weeks in a tiny space like this with a man who got angry easily!

"Oh, Nigel, Nigel!"

Flame flung herself face downwards onto her berth.

When she came round to a realization of ordinary things again, she found she had been to sleep, and that a steward was standing by her bed.

"A cup of tea, sir," this kind man had said.

He handed it to her with a plate of biscuits.

Tea had restored her a little; and, finished, she had carried the cup and plate outside and put them on a grating.

Then, seeing the deck fairly deserted, she had started to walk up and down. It was heavenly cool, in fact, almost cold. Like a drowning man clutching at a straw, she had rushed in to get her Burberry, and had then felt much happier, her slim legs concealed.

So the exercise had done her good, and when the ever-active deck steward had approached her with an armful of rugs, she had cheerfully asked him what time dinner would be.

"Half-past seven, sir."

"What time do the people generally start dressing for dinner?" questioned Flame anxiously.

"Oh, from half-past six onwards, sir."

"Oh, I see."

Flame glanced at the silver watch on her wrist. It was nearly six now. She must begin, otherwise that dreadful man would be coming up to change.

So she walked as carelessly as she could to her own cabin, and, once inside, flung herself passionately on the door and locked and bolted it.

She had got to the shirt stage when there was a sharp rap outside. It was Mr Keymer's voice, rather impatient.

"Open the door, will you? I want to get a couple of books."

"I can't, I'm not properly dressed," answered Flame, suddenly pallid.

"Never mind that, I shan't be a second."

There was an awful silence. Flame could hear Mr Keymer clearing his throat. Then he spoke again, more quietly this time.

"Look here, you're not supposed to lock your cabin door. Open it at once, please."

"I can't!"

Flame had her hands held tightly over her breast.

"Damn you, do what you're told!"

Mr Keymer rattled the handle. Flame, terrified at this, cried out. "I will. Oh, wait a minute ... wait a minute!"

How often in after-years Hugh Keymer laughed tenderly as he thought of that shrinking little figure in the bathgown crushed up against the end of the berth; but now he was annoyed and he walked into the cabin trying not to show it.

He took two books out of the rack.

"Hurry up with your dressing. I shall be back in about another ten minutes."

"I don't know if I shall be quite ready by then," returned Flame, thinking in a frenzy of the ties that she had not been able to find.

Hunting for them had delayed her; she had had to go twice through the suit-cases as well as through the things in the drawers. Fancy if she had left them at the Strand Palace Hotel!

What would she do, what should she do? ...

"Well, I shan't be more than ten minutes," said Hugh.

He turned on his heel and went out of the door. But he was back before Flame had done more than look through one suit-case. She lifted her face, pale with anxiety.

"I can't find my dress-tie."

"I think I have a spare one."

Hugh Keymer looked with amusement at the small slight figure in shirt and trousers. The kid had got one of the loops of the braces twisted.

"Here you are."

He opened a drawer, took out a narrow black strip and threw it across the cabin.

"But it isn't ready tied," exclaimed Flame, as she looked at it lying in her hand.

"No, I should hope it isn't."

He had taken off his coat and was settling it on a wooden hanger.

"Don't start undressing until I've gone," Flame cried out, flushing all over her small pointed face.

Hugh Keymer turned round and stared. The kid must be mad; he came to the conclusion swiftly. He would go to the purser the next day and find out a little about him. Meanwhile he would humour him.

"Very well."

He sat good-temperedly down on the edge of the berth and waited.

Flame advanced to the glass, the tie in her hand. How did you tie a dress-tie? she wondered uneasily.

It looked easy enough when Nigel did it, but sometimes those easy-looking things were the most difficult.

She slipped it round her neck, and pulled the ends even.

"I say, don't ruin it!"

Hugh Keymer spoke after two minutes of intensest irritation. He had made up his mind not to say anything, but it was too much for him. Besides, he only had two black evening ties with him.

"I can't do it," faltered Flame.

In the mirror Hugh Keymer could see the small face working.

"Let me do it for you, then?"

Hugh Keymer got up and strolled to the glass. "Oh, thank you!"

Flame swung round, her face alight with joy and relief.

"Now, turn your back to me, it's easier to tie a bow tie on somebody else if they're not facing you."

Flame turned obediently. Hugh, behind her, strained the tie carefully round the collar and then, with a couple of deft twists, tied an excellent bow.

Flame watched him excitely in the mirror.

"I say, you do do it well!" she exclaimed.

"Long practice," returned Hugh Keymer, who under pretext of adjusting the bow to the exact middle of the collar was scrutinizing the face below his in the glass.

There was something about it—what was it? Flame lifted her little white chin.

"Has anyone told you what an awfully nice face you've got?" she said.

She smiled up into the mirrored eyes.

Hugh Keymer was taken aback. He dropped his hands and turned on his heel, ignoring the question.

"Here, don't go without your waistcoat," he said, as Flame, after a couple of minutes' agonized fumbling with her coat, stood upright in it.

"I've annoyed you by saying that about your face," stammered Flame, not hearing the remark about the coat.

"Oh no, it's all right." But Hugh Keymer spoke very shortly. He would certainly get the kid shifted. "Put on your waist coat."

"Oh, haven't I got it on?"

Flame spoke with tears in her eyes. There was something about this man that had given her a wonderful warm, comforting feeling in her soul. Now he was frowning.

"No, you haven't."

But as he spoke, a little impatiently, Hugh had his eyes on the little face again. What was it? he wondered.

Hugh Keymer came to bed very late. He had been drawn into a man's Bridge four. He came into the cabin very quietly.

But Flame was awake.

She had fallen asleep at first, and had then waked wondering where she was, and the newness and the strangeness of it all had stabbed anew into her soul.

"Nigel, Nigel!" The words came out in an overwhelming flood of homesickness.

Hugh Keymer stopped, his finger on the electric switch.

He had made up his mind as he came up the stairs that he would not grope about the cabin in the dark; let the kid take his chance if he had already gone to bed.

But at the sound of his sobs his heart melted and he took his hand down; so had he sobbed in the old days on his first night back at school.

"I say, don't give it up," he said, and very kindly he sat down on the end of the narrow berth. "We all know what it is to leave home for the first time. Tell me about it; it may make you feel better."

But Flame, startled and terrified, burrowed lower into the blankets. The man coming to bed!

What would people think? Nigel for instance.

"I'm all right," she choked.

She turned a little in a wild effort for self-control, and looked up at the face seen dimly close to hers.

Hugh Keymer was touched at the sudden struggle with obviously overmastering misery, and he put out a kind hand.

"Tell me a little about it all," he said, and he laid his hand on what he thought would be a shoulder.

But it was not, and Hugh Keymer stood abruptly upright. There was a palpitating silence.

Then Flame, quite unconscious, spoke:

"You see, it's the desperate loneliness of it," she said, and as she spoke she rolled over and faced the cabin. "That's what I mind so much. I've got a twin brother, and although he goes to school we always seem as if we belong to each other."

She gave a little gulp.

"And now I seem to be getting farther and farther away from him; in fact, I am getting farther and farther away."

Hugh Keymer did not answer. He was staring blankly out into the darkness. What in the name of Heaven was he to do?

Keep quiet, he came to the conclusion swiftly. But in the meantime . . . And he slid a seeking foot round the cabin, located the carpet stool, and opening it, drew it up close to the bed.

Then he sat down on it, linking his hands loosely in front of him.

"Look here. Don't cry anymore, men don't cry. Keep a stiff upper lip, and things will be better in the morning. And meanwhile, try and go to sleep. It's very late."

"I'm sleepy now!"

Through the darkness Hugh heard a little yawn, like the creak of a kitten's pink jaws.

"Good. Just roll over and shut your eyes then."

"I wish you would sit by me till I am off," said Flame.

Hugh, sitting very still, felt with alarm the groping of a soft hand on his knee.

"I should like to take hold of your hand too; it would give me a heavenly comforted feeling inside. You've got that sort of a face too, a sort of understanding face. I saw it in Westminster Abbey.

"Do you think it would matter if I did take hold of your hand, or would it be the sort of thing that a man of my age would never do?"

"Oh, I don't think it would matter!"

Hugh's lean brown hand closed on the softly groping one.

"You see, I'm very old compared to you."

"How old?"

"Thirty-seven," he replied wearily.

"Oh, I say, how old!" Flame spoke in consternation.

"Yes, it's desperate, isn't it?"

His weariness broke up into laughter.

"Now I hold your hand I feel that heavenly sleepy feeling creeping all over me," said Flame drowsily. "Stay a minute or two more, will you?"

"Yes, I will, certainly," said Hugh Keymer.

He sat until the clasp of the soft little fingers relaxed and the breath came slow and evenly from between the parted lips.

Then he got up, and tucking his pyjamas under his arm, tiptoed along to the bathroom.

But all the same, back in his cabin again, in spite of his calm acceptance of what was indubitably a fact, Hugh Keymer took a very long time to go to sleep.

He could hear Flame's soft even breathing and once or twice she caught her breath in a long sobbing sigh. It was not an easy situation, even to a man as much of the world as Hugh Keymer.

Who was she?—that was the question that occupied him to the exclusion of everything else at the moment. Gently bred, apparently, but then, you could never tell.

What should he do?

Keep quiet! He came to the conclusion after ten minutes' profound thought. Keep quiet, at any rate until they were getting near to Marseilles.

Then if he found that it was necessary he could inform the authorities and she could be sent to the nearest Girls' Friendly Society.

But meanwhile—and Hugh Keymer's mouth twitched—he was in command of the situation, and "Master" Peterson must be made to remember it.

Hugh Keymer rolled blithely over on to his side and went to sleep.

Chapter
Four

"Well, this is pretty gorgeous, isn't it?"

Hugh Keymer, his face stinging from the spray that from time to time fell on the upper deck with a rattle of small shot, dropped his long length in a vacant chair beside Hester Lane.

"Um-m-m." Dr Lane was lying at full length in her chair and was well covered up with a rug. She turned her head rather carefully.

"Good Heavens! you don't mean to say you feel this?"

"Not as long as I keep still. But to see you going so joyfully up and down the deck . . ." Dr Lane shuddered.

"I say, I am sorry—let me get you something."

Hugh Keymer's delightful face was instantly all sympathy.

"No, no; I'm perfectly all right, really. How is our little mad friend?" Dr Lane laughed quietly.

"Feeling rather sorry for himself." Hugh Keymer flung his back in his chair and laughed. "But I made him get up and have a bath. It was a brutal thing to do really, but I knew it would be better for him in the end."

"You brute!"

But Hester Lane's eyes were soft. How heavenly to be really looked after by this man, she was thinking, to be in his cabin, close to him.

Yet the woman who bore his name, what was she doing at this moment?

Probably staring with brooding, bloodshot eyes out of her window, cursing the day when she had consented to enter the ruinously expensive Home where the Mrs Keymers of this world are catered for.

The wife of this man!

Oh, the ghastly, hideous shame of it!

"I'm not really a brute, you know, Hester."

Hugh Keymer had suddenly the look of a shy boy as he glanced across the small space that separated the two chairs.

Hester Lane's eyes suddenly filled.

"You need not tell me that, Hugh," she said.

She drew a hand from under the rug and laid it on the lean brown one close to hers. There was a little silence.

Both were thinking of the same thing: the voyage when they had got to know one another, quite a long time ago now, ten years.

Hester had seemed much older than Hugh then, but he had aged more quickly than she, although indeed, she had always been about five years his senior.

It had been on the return voyage from Nairobi they had met, Hugh Keymer, the biographer, suddenly sprung into fame for his daring though sympathetic life of King Edward.

He had been travelling with his wife, a little faded thing like a mouse, with lips tightly folded.

They were an odd couple, never apart; for hours they would sit together on deck.

One day in the Red Sea he had gone down with what the ship's doctor had pronounced to be influenza, and Mrs Keymer had sat alone.

That night Hester, passing along the white painted corridor to her own cabin, had surprised Hugh Keymer swaying against the lintel of the door, clutching the serge curtain, his eyes blazing with fever.

"My wife, where is she?" he had gasped.

He was quite unconscious of what he was saying, except that he knew that he was speaking to the woman with quite steady eyes who was a doctor.

Hester had first deposited him safely on his berth with the steady grasp of the born physician, then promised to go and find out.

Indeed she had found out.

Mrs Keymer, the ceaseless vigilance of her husband relaxed, had signed for a bottle of whisky, and was lying dead-drunk under one of the saloon dining-tables.

That was the beginning of a very beautiful friendship. Hester Lane felt like a mother over the agonized man. She and the stewardess kept the secret well.

When they landed at Tilbury, the woman with serious eyes and the tall man gripped hands and promised to meet again.

They did, many times, and lately Hester had been largely instrumental in getting Mrs Keymer into the Home in which she now was.

"Well, how do you feel?"

Hugh Keymer stood in the door of the cabin looking down at the little figure under the blankets. How could he ever have thought that this little creature was anything else but a girl?

"Much better," said Flame.

"Good! Are you going to get up?"

"I don't know about that," Flame answered.

She twisted a little sideways on her berth and stared up doubtfully.

Hugh Keymer averted his gaze. But there was something in him which seized on and chuckled over the situation; it was a racy one, and one that might develop very entertainingly.

"Well," he said, "I advise you to get up, anyhow. I shall be doing my mile up and down the deck. Give me a shout if you want any help."

"All right," said Flame, and she smiled fleetingly. "Will you tie my tie?"

"I will, certainly."

"All right then, I'll call you when I have got to that," said Flame.

Very, very shyly she began to struggle her feet from under the sheet.

After all, as she thought swiftly, she must behave as if she didn't think anything of having a man in her cabin.

But Hugh had gone, backing swiftly through the curtain the moment she began to move.

Mrs Holroyd-Browne liked the company of young boys, it made her feel younger.

"Hallo, you sweet thing!" she hailed Flame, who had just emerged from the companion door, very rosy and trim in white flannel trousers and blue blazer.

Flame had now quite got her sea-legs, and was beginning to enjoy herself terrifically. She was in the wildest spirits, and she returned Mrs Holroyd-Browne's salutation with enthusiasm.

"You seem very pleased with yourself," said Mrs Holroyd-Browne.

She looked with what was really tragic envy at the incarnation of youth in front of her.

"I am," said Flame, "aren't you?"

She sat down on the white-boards of the deck and crossed her legs.

"Now I am," said Mrs Holroyd-Browne meaningly.

"Why? Because I have come to sit by you? You dear," said Flame.

She thrilled with a wild longing to laugh.

"Yes, that's why," said Mrs Holroyd-Browne.

"But how sweet of you," said Flame.

She put out a soft young hand and gave the rather hard one an impulsive squeeze.

"Now, now," said Mrs Holroyd-Browne warningly, and she held up a finger.

"Why, what have I said?" asked Flame, with a look of sweetest innocence.

But inwardly her heart was singing.

"Fun, fun, fun!" she was chuckling to herself. "Oh, what frantic fun this is!"

"Why, a boy like you must not say those things to an old woman like me," replied Mrs Holroyd-Browne.

"Why not? Besides, you're not old at all, you're quite young," put in Flame audaciously.

She jumped abruptly up.

"Oh, I'm sorry I can't stay any longer now," she said, "but I see Mr Keymer, and I believe he is getting names for the sports."

Hugh Keymer was the centre of a group of very young men when Flame came up. There were a good many young civilians going out to India.

"I want to go in for the sports, can I?"

Flame's eager face, on a level with his shoulder, smiled up into Hugh Keymer's face.

"The sports! Hm-m."

Hugh was sitting at a small table, a writing-block in front of him.

"Which do you want to go in for?"

"All of them!" said Flame, with a delighted kick.

Hugh dropped his eyes, full of intensest merriment.

Really, it was tremendous fun to see this child finding her feet. Not a soul suspected, that was obvious. For one or two of the young men were already staring contemptuously.

Peterson was a conceited young ass, always hanging about a woman old enough to be his mother. For Mrs Holroyd-Browne's preference for the boy with yellow hair and black eyebrows was already beginning to be the talk of the ship.

"How about the egg-and-spoon race?" he said.

"Why, that's a girl's thing!"

Flame's voice was full of contempt.

"Not entirely; you have to choose a girl for a partner, I admit, but that's all. Yes, I'll put you down for that."

Hugh scribbled with relief. This was going

to be difficult. The child could not compete with men. But Flame was full of excitement, and burning to live up to her role.

"And all the other things?" she asked.

"Most of them are full up."

Hugh glanced casually down the list.

"Isn't there any jumping?"

"What sort of jumping?"

Hugh's eyes were very clear and steady as he lifted them from the sheets of paper in front of him.

"Oh, jumping over things," said Flame.

Then for some extraordinary reason her own eyes wavered and fell before the clear ones.

What was it? . . .

These eyes weren't like other people's eyes. They had something behind them, something that made you feel . . . made you feel . . . made you feel what? Like a girl.

Flame came to the conclusion swiftly and with burning cheeks.

Hugh dropped his eyes again. Did she suspect that her secret was no longer her own? he wondered.

But he need not have wondered; such a thought was miles from Flame's mind. It had only been a funny sort of feeling that she had had, just for a minute.

And now it had gone! Only a sort of thumpy feeling in her heart was still there, and that would go directly.

"Yes, jumping over things," she went on, "put me down for that, will you?"

"No, that's all full," said Hugh calmly.

"But how can it be? You've only just sat

down here to take the names of people," Flame
said indignantly.

"Really, that is very interesting information.
But who runs the Sports Committee, you or I?"

"You do . . . but . . ."

Flame broke off. There was the same look in
the steady eyes. She felt the tell-tale colour stealing
down from behind her ears.

"Exactly, and therefore I decide who shall
compete and who shall not. And now, if I might
suggest it, I should say that it would be a good
thing if you would go and tidy your cabin."

"It is tidy!" Flame was blazing.

"Not what I call tidy: you've left your pyjamas unfolded."

Hugh's face was grave although his eyes were
dancing.

"Have I?"

Flame's face was scarlet again. She turned to
go.

As she turned, a gentle hand touched her
arm. She swung round and met a pair of faltering
blue eyes.

"If you are going in for the egg-and-spoon
race, may I be your partner?" said Mary Ashe, terrified out of her life at having made the first ad-
vance.

But Mr Peterson was so frightfully good-
looking, and it wasn't fair that the old lady should
have him all to herself.

"Oh, all right, I mean certainly!"

Flame, taken completely by surprise, tried
wildly to remember how Nigel would have spoken
to a young, pretty girl like this.

Then it all came back to her.

"Of course," she said. "How extremely nice of you to ask me."

It was most frantic fun this, making grown-up people look squirmy, Flame thought. Not that Mary Ashe could be more than seventeen. But then that was grown up.

Flame, dressed for her first dance, filled with the wildest excitement. If only Mr Keymer would hurry up and come up to dress; she wanted her tie tied.

"Oh joy, I thought you weren't ever coming!"

Flame, very slim and small in trousers and pleated shirt, was standing in the middle of the tiny carpeted space as Hugh Keymer lounged into it.

"What's the matter? Want your tie tied, or rather, want my tie tied?" said Hugh with significant emphasis.

"Oh yes, of course; I forgot it was yours," said Flame, rather crestfallen. "But perhaps we could get one at Gibraltar tomorrow."

"Probably! Anyhow, we needn't bother about that now. Come here, if you want it done, before you put your collar on," said Hugh.

"Half a second!" she said.

Hugh watched her. Such a little white neck, and such useless little hands.

What else could she be but a girl, he thought, and how could anyone mistake it for anything else?

He watched, amused, as Flame, having retrieved a clean collar, started putting it round her neck from the wrong side.

"Shall I help?" he asked, after a long pause,

during which Flame fought unavailingly with the heavily starched buttonhole.

"Oh, it's desperately stiff!"

"Come, come! Don't lose your temper!"

. But inwardly Hugh was in convulsions of laughter. He got up from his stool and picked up the offending strip of linen.

"Now then," he said, and then frowned. "Your back stud's gone."

"Gone! Where?"

"I don't know, probably either on to the floor or down your back. Try the floor first, there's heaps of time."

Hugh sat down on the stool again, the collar still in his hand, as Flame, dismayed, went down on her knees.

"It isn't here!"

Flame, after a prolonged search, crouched round on her heels and spoke hopelessly.

"Very well then, I'll try your back. Stand up straight."

Hugh got up and towered over her.

"No, you can't!"

Flame was still crouching, and she flung out her hands.

"Can't? Of course I can. Hurry up, there's the first bugle."

Hugh's eyes were inscrutable, although in the depths of them something danced.

"If you wouldn't mind looking the other way I will just pull out my shirt, and then it may either fall out or run down my leg," said Flame.

Her breath began to come faster as she got slowly on to her feet.

"I don't in the least mind seeing you pull out

your shirt," said Hugh, and his hand wandered up to his own tie.

"But I'll go on with my own dressing meanwhile, if you don't mind, as it's getting late."

"Lord, what am I to do?"

Flame stood with clenched hands and prayed.

This was discovery, for she could neither let this tall man with searching eyes put a hand down her back nor go on undressing.

Something cold ran swiftly down behind her knees.

"Oh, it's come!" she almost screamed.

"Good!" And Hugh Keymer spoke with a certain amount of relief.

After all, as he thought, this was hardly the moment to get it out of her, although he would have done so in another five minutes.

He picked up the tiny round of mother-of-pearl from the carpet and twisted her round with a firm, lean hand.

Flame enjoyed herself immensely at the dance, being pursued by Mary Ashe and Mrs Holroyd-Browne. She thought it a huge joke that neither of them guessed she was a girl.

But Hugh Keymer, against the rail, a cigarette between his lips, watched the two young figures with distaste.

For the last three days he had seen that little soft Ashe child following Peterson about with her eyes; now there was that Holroyd-Browne woman making a fool of herself over him.

It had got to be stopped, and at once, before anything worse happened.

"Hallo, here you are!"

The girls had not heard the quiet step beside them.

"Oh, it's Mr Keymer!" Flame's voice was choked with terror.

"Yes, it is. Come along with me, Peterson, will you please? Or rather, wait here for me, while I take Miss Ashe back to her mother. Don't move from here."

Flame waited, her heart beating in anguish. What had she done to make him angry? she asked herself.

Very soon the tall figure was back again, breathing a little quickly too.

"Come along up to the cabin," he said roughly.

Flame followed him, terrified.

Hugh Keymer dragged the curtain across behind him with a fierce hand, and fumbled in the bag of golf clubs standing in the corner.

"What are you going to do?" Flame had turned absolutely white.

"Give you what you deserve. Men don't single out young girls in the dark after three days' acquaintance. Take off your coat."

Hugh stood, coatless himself, a thin cane in his hand.

"But she half asked me to." Flame's eyes were dark with fear.

"Don't make it worse. Take off your coat," he said again.

Flame took it off with hands almost paralysed with fear. What should she do?

"Will you hit me very hard?" she quavered.

"Probably," and Hugh took a couple of steps forward, his face was like stone.

She was going too far, with this pretence of hers. Well, he would have the truth out of her now.

"But . . . but you can't," she gasped.

"And why not?" he retorted.

"Because . . . because . . ."

Then Flame's control broke down, and she flung herself on her berth in a storm of sobs.

Hugh waited for a minute or two and then spoke.

"Stop it," he said harshly.

"I can't!" Flame stuffed a corner of the pillow into her mouth.

"Yes, you can. Stop it!" he said again.

"You don't understand," she cried.

She got slowly off the berth.

"I'm not a boy at all, I'm a girl," she sobbed.

She fell on her knees at Hugh's feet and caught hold of his legs.

"I knew that before you'd been in this ship twelve hours," said Hugh Keymer.

He spoke dryly and stared with hard eyes at Flame's bathgown that swung out a little on the brass hook.

"You knew it!"

Flame's swollen eyes were wide with fear, and she clutched Hugh's knees with fingers that shook.

"Of course I did. Let go of me and get up."

"Now you'll tell somebody."

"Probably! I ought to have done so long ago."

"No, no, don't! Nigel said that they would put me in prison or a reformatory or something. Promise me, promise me!"

"Tell me who you are then, and tell me without lying about it."

Hugh's eyes had softened a little, but he still spoke harshly.

"I will, I will!" Flame struggled up on to her feet.

"I will tell you everything, only let me tell you quietly, and not with you looking at me like that. Otherwise I can't get it all straight in my head."

"Very well, begin," said Hugh, and then he hesitated.

"No, wait a minute. It will be better for me to go back again and come up later. You get undressed and get into bed, and I'll come back in about half an hour."

But Flame hung her head, and over her face a very deep flush slowly spread.

"It makes it rather different undressing, now that you know I'm a girl."

Hugh's reply came in a very still, icy voice.

"I don't see that, it makes not the faintest difference to me what you are, provided you behave yourself. Besides, I am a married man."

"Oh, you are?" exclaimed Flame eagerly. "Have you got any children about my age?"

"No," replied Hugh stonily.

Long after midnight they were still talking, Flame sitting up on her berth, her little thin arms round her pyjamaed legs, and Hugh still in evening clothes, a pipe between his teeth and his eyes incredulous.

"But what about your people?" he said. "They will surely raise Cain when they find you have gone. Your mother . . ."

"Mother will be glad," said Flame.

"But does nobody but your brother and your butler know?"

"Gerald knows," said Flame.

"And who is Gerald?"

"Gerald is Colonel Forsythe," said Flame, "and I adore him."

"Oh, really," and Hugh's voice suddenly went cold.

This then was at the bottom of the broken engagement with the elderly peer; he thought there was something that did not ring quite true about that.

"Yes," said Flame fervently. "I owe almost everything in the world to Gerald."

She went on to tell him how Gerald had helped her.

Hugh was silent for a minute or two. Then he spoke.

"Come here."

"Not to beat me?" Flame spoke breathlessly.

"No. Stand here, close, where I can see you. That's it," as Flame advanced timorously across the cabin.

"Now then," and he took hold of the little white chin and held it. "Now then, look straight up into my eyes until I tell you that you may move."

"How much longer?" faltered Flame, after a quivering silence.

"No longer, that's enough." Hugh dropped his lean fingers to his side.

It was innocence; unmistakable; what on earth was he to do? Confide in Hester, it was the only thing to be done. And meanwhile . . .

"Hop into bed, and good night."

"Oh . . . why, aren't you coming back?" Flame cried, dismayed.

She stood in the middle of the carpeted space, her hands clasped dejectedly in front of her.

"Why, I love feeling you close to me, it makes me seem so absolutely safe."

"Does it? Well, I'm glad," said Hugh dryly. "But I'm afraid it isn't possible anymore. You see, the P & O had old-fashioned ideas about people sharing cabins, and it likes to keep its men and women separate."

"But then, are you going to *tell* anybody?" said Flame, and she made a wild little rush across the floor.

"No, not really," said Hugh, and he caught the two trembling little hands and held them close. "Anyhow, not anyone who will interfere. Now then, into bed, and don't worry.

"And look here, I'm sorry I gave you a fright; only, you see, I thought it was about time to end your little game, at any rate as far as we were concerned."

"Oh, I see."

Flame dropped her head, and then lifted it again.

"I suppose you couldn't kiss me to show that you are really sorry, could you? It's something about your eyes and the way you hold my hands that makes me feel most heavenly all over.

"Do you know the feeling you get when you are in a very hot bath, all sort of tingly? Well, it's like that."

Hugh shook his head.

"Nothing doing," he said, but his lips were twitching uncontrollably. "Hop into bed, Master Nigel. The P & O would have us flung overboard if they found that we were kissing in their precious cabins."

"Would they? Oh, I see!"

Flame was suddenly grave.

"Better not do it then. Only call me by my proper name, please do, just once for good night. 'Flame' is my name, do you like it?"

"Very much indeed," said Hugh gravely. "Good night, Miss Flame."

"Good night," said Flame.

All her innocent heart was shining out of her grey eyes.

Hester Lane was incensed, incensed and outraged.

A girl masquerading as a boy and sharing a cabin with a man!

"Hugh, you must report it instantly."

"Must I?"

Hugh Keymer suddenly got a funny obstinate look on his nice mouth.

"Yes, of course you must! Why, I can't understand why you haven't done it long ago. It's . . . it's . . . awful. Hugh! Why, it's . . . it's revolting."

Dr. Lane's usually serene face was all furrowed.

"Why revolting?" Hugh spoke with a quiet smile.

"Well, of course it is. Undressing and dressing in a cabin with a man. Even saying it makes me feel revolted."

"But she doesn't, she waits until I go away." Hugh laughed.

"Don't laugh, you make me furious."

"Then I'm sorry I told you. But I thought you'd see things with rather a broader view. I admit that the situation lacks regularity, but when you've said that you've said all. Miss Flame, rather a sweet name, by the way, is perfectly safe with me."

Hester Lane sat back in her deck-chair and tried to subdue the extraordinary turmoil of sensation in which she was engulfed.

Hugh would fall in love with her, with this designing little minx who had thrust herself in his way, *but he should not!*

Flame was very miserable for the next few days as Hugh kept her in her cabin most of the time.

She felt she had to confide in someone or she would burst.

That night, as the saloon passengers were coming out from dinner, she slipped a little ahead of Dr Lane.

Dr Lane always walked out beside her if Mr Keymer didn't. Flame was beginning to hate the quiet controlled face.

She touched Mary Ashe swiftly on her bare elbow.

"I want to say something to you," she said.

"Mother says I'm not to speak to you," Mary Ashe replied at once.

Her mouth trembled as she met the pleading grey eyes.

"I must, I shall go mad if I can't."

"But how can I? Mother will find out and be furious."

"Come along, Nigel." It was Dr Lane's voice, very quiet and resolved, and it roused every atom of opposition in Flame.

"Meet me outside my cabin in half an hour," she whispered.

"All right," and Mary Ashe had gone.

Like a frightened rabbit, she burrowed into the little crowd ahead of her.

So a little later Flame, strolling up and down outside her cabin, heard a soft hesitating step, and she flung round and caught the soft hands in hers. There was no one about.

Flame drew the little figure down on to a seat and flung her arm round it.

"Oh, Mary, how I love you for coming! Don't tremble like that, there's nothing to tremble at. I want to tell you something most frantically, frantically secret. Can you keep a secret?"

"Yes," said Mary.

"Well, I'm not a boy at all, I'm a girl," said Flame abruptly.

There was a little silence.

Then Mary seemed to stiffen and she drew herself away.

"But . . ." she stammered, "but . . . I thought . . . I . . . oh, how could you . . . how could you!"

She tore herself from Flame's encircling arm, and broke into dreadful, rending sobs.

"Mary," said Flame, "listen, you must listen. You must. When I've told you everything you'll see I simply couldn't have done anything else. Really I couldn't."

"All right," said Mary, beginning to control herself, "but I shall *never, never* forgive you."

But when Flame had told her story, looking so terribly young and innocent and unprotected, Mary's soft little heart melted after all.

"Now you know *everything*," Flame ended up, "it does make a difference, doesn't it?"

"Well, I rather think it does," said Mary, after a very long tremulous pause.

All Flame's usual elasticity returned.

"Now I feel much happier because I have told you. Oh, it's a joy to be able to confide in someone! Vow, vow you will never tell a soul. You said you could keep a secret: can you really?"

"Yes, I really can," said Mary, and she spoke the truth. "But oh, Nigel, do tell me more about it; where did you get the clothes and everything?"

"I will tell you, only call me Flame, not Nigel, that's my name. Oh, I'm dying to tell you; come closer and I will. Only I'm going to tell you the end part first, because that's the most heavenly part. Well . . ."

Flame flung a gentle arm round the soft waist.

"You know I have a cabin up here, just along that passage it is. Well, I share it with a man . . ."

"Mr Keymer?" breathed Mary.

"Yes."

"Oh, how I envy you!" Mary's breath came from between parted lips.

"Yes . . . I knew you'd understand: isn't it bliss? Heavenly, heavenly bliss!"

Flame rocked herself a little and made a soft cooing noise in her throat.

"Does he think it's bliss too?" asked Mary.

"No, I don't know that he does," replied Flame, and her soft face fell in the darkness.

"I expect he does," said Mary staunchly, all aglow for this wonderful new friend of hers.

"No, because if he did he'd have to show it sometimes," said Flame, and she caught her breath a little.

"I am sure he must like it," repeated Mary staunchly. "There is something about you that any man would like, something cuddly and soft. Your hands are soft and rather trembly, and your eyes are sort of simple; do you know what I mean?

"And your mouth is so red . . . Oh, Flame!

Do tell me how you came to dress up like a boy, and all about it, will you?"

"Yes, I will sometime, but not now. Now, I only want to tell you about how I feel about Mr Keymer. It's the most extraordinary feeling . . ."

Flame propped her chin on her hands and stared out into the darkness.

"It's the sort of feeling that when I see him all my inside jumps up, do you know? Then just about here . . ."

Mary, watching, saw two small hands falter to each side of the black roll collar.

"I feel a sort of creeping feeling. Then I get an empty feeling, do you know, like when you've been out in the garden before breakfast."

"Go on," breathed Mary.

"Well, it's awful," went on Flame. "It's awful because it's always going on, and it makes me so tired. And it isn't as if he ever smiled at me, or anything like that; he only just *is*, do you know what I mean?

"All the time something inside me is surging out to try and make him take some sort of kind notice of me, and he won't, he won't!"

Flame suddenly broke down and began to cry.

"Don't cry, darling Flame!" Mary's sweet face was tender through the darkness.

"I must cry because I am so wretched," sobbed Flame. "Besides, all the time I've got a creeping terror all over me that when we get to Port Said he is going to have me sent home. I heard something . . . Dr Lane knows about my being a girl."

"But don't you want to go home?" said Mary wonderingly.

"No, of course I don't . . . how can I? I only want to be with him."

Flame wept anew.

"But haven't you got a mother?" Mary's voice was wondering.

"Yes, I have, but I don't care for her very much," sobbed Flame.

"Oh, poor Flame, how awful!"

This roused all Mary's tenderest sympathy. Not to care for your mother, how perfectly frightful! She gathered the sobbing figure closer to her.

"I love my brother, but somehow, now it all seems so feeble compared to this new feeling."

Flame was still sobbing hopelessly as she said, "This feeling makes me feel mad and frantic; I want to crawl out of my berth and get into his and have him hold me tight in his arms. But he isn't in his berth now; he's gone away to sleep somewhere else. . . ."

"Perhaps he knows you feel like that," breathed Mary, awestruck.

"Yes, perhaps he does . . . anyhow, I do, I do, and I can't help it!"

Flame got up, and struck one small clenched fist against the other.

Mary Ashe also got up. She was a little more versed in the ways of the world than Flame, although only a very little more. But her gentle heart was anxious.

Flame must not prejudice her chances with this very nice man by doing anything funny like getting into his berth. People didn't do that . . . at least, Mary felt pretty sure that they didn't.

"And he has a wife . . . that makes me feel more frantic than anything," stormed on Flame.

"A wife! Oh, Flame!" Mary went suddenly rigid.

"A wife!"

Then all this was deadly, deadly sin.

"Flame, if he has a wife, you must stop thinking about him at once."

"Stop thinking about him!" Flame stood suddenly stock-still. "Stop thinking about him, Mary? But I love him . . . I tell you that I love him!"

As Flame said this the most heavenly radiance spread all over her face.

That was it then, this glorious feeling that swept you off your feet and left you quivering in the air; it was love. Love!

"Mary, I have fallen in love," she said, and her voice was a benediction.

"You can't fall in love with a married man," said Mary indignantly.

She laid two trembling hands on her bursting throat. "But I have done!" said Flame.

Chapter
Five

It was the flash of crossed swords that passed between the two chairs; then Hester Lane got up.

"Then there is nothing more to be said," she said, and her voice was trembling.

"Yes there is, a good deal. Sit down again, Hester."

Hugh's voice was steady, although the hands thrust deep into his pockets were not.

"Sustain your argument with something tangible; you haven't done so yet. All you reiterate is that it is my duty to have Miss Peterson sent home from Port Said. Well . . ."

"You know it is your duty, Hugh!"

Hester Lane's eyes were blazing.

"How do I know it?" Hugh Keymer's voice was intentionally lazy.

"Because everything that is decent within you ought to tell you so," replied Hester furiously.

She dropped eyes dark with misery to the neglected knitting on her lap.

"Decency and I parted company long since,"

he said slowly. "I want diversion, Hester. Can you blame me if I take advantage of it?"

"Hugh you make me . . . you make me . . ." Hester's voice was strange.

"Yes, of course I do, because you have no idea really of a man's true nature. Decency, as you reckon it, in a man is only a veneer. Underneath we're all alike, wild animals," and Hugh laughed shortly.

"Miss Peterson has a mother . . . her proper place is with her."

Hester Lane's rather large, hard hands were twisted painfully together.

"No, there I think you're wrong."

Hugh slipped a brown hand into the inner pocket of his blazer.

"Look here, it was Marconied from Malta."

He handed across the paper of badly printed Reuter's telegrams.

"It may be only a coincidence, of course, but the name is not a common one."

Hester Lane read swiftly. A very ordinary occurrence really, an overdose of veronal at a London hotel. She returned the paper silently.

"Well?"

"Does she know?"

"No."

"Well, you had better let me tell her." Hester spoke with an effort.

"No, I will. Besides, we don't know yet if it is her mother at all." Hugh replaced the paper, carefully folded, in his pocket.

"Very well, do what you like," she said after a while, and her voice was strained and old.

"But I warn you, Hugh, that if you persist

in this, to me, inexplicably lax way of thinking, I shall feel it my duty to inform the authorities in this ship of Miss Peterson's true identity."

"You will do nothing of the kind!"

Hugh turned his head sharply, and there was a fierce look on his nice mouth.

"I shall. I ought to have done it long ago." Dr Lane held her head high.

"The secret was mine, and like a fool I confided it to you, trusting you."

Hugh had got up, and his shaking hands were driven deep into his pockets.

"I don't care, I mean to save you from yourself." Hester's eyes were steady.

"Pah, don't be a fool! Save me from myself, what do you mean? You speak as if I were in love with Miss Peterson."

Hugh had forced a careless laugh on to his lips, and he also forced himself to stare steadily at the woman opposite him.

"You are . . . you know you are."

Hester made one dying clutch at self-control and common sense and then let them go, once and for all.

"I can see it in the way you look at her, speak to her, speak of her. She has wormed herself into your heart; under the guise of innocence and immaturity, she has infatuated you.

"All this pretended reticence about sharing a cabin with you . . . it is put on. What does she care, what does she care if you do go in while she is half undressed? She likes it . . . probably that is what she is aiming at, to get you to do it so that she—"

"Be quiet, Hester."

"No, I shall not be quiet. Hugh, you are a married man. Pull yourself together before it is too late."

Hester's eyes had begun to stream.

"Sit down and be quiet."

Hugh Keymer cast a swift glance around him. No, mercifully they were fairly isolated.

"Look here, you've got this all wrong," he said kindly.

He sat down and took the shaking hands in his.

"If according to your particular code I am in danger of hell-fire because I choose to befriend a charming and innocent child, leave me to burn. It doesn't affect you after all, does it?"

"Ah, but it does, it does!"

And Hester Lane dropped her face into her hands and shed the bitterest tears that had ever scorched their way out from between her eyelids.

But Hugh had dropped the rather heavy hands and had stood up. No, this was beyond a joke. He suddenly felt a wild desire to stop Hester from saying what she would probably spend the rest of her life in regretting.

Hester Lane heard him get on to his feet and stood up, too, facing him.

She bit back the words that had so nearly forced utterance. But the biting back had bred bitterness, and she spoke without an atom of relenting in her voice.

"I shall feel it my duty to inform the captain of what I know," she said.

"You are not to do it." Hugh's voice was furious.

"I am sorry, but I feel I must."

"If you do it, it is absolutely the end of everything in the way of friendship between us."

Hugh's voice was steadier now, and he only looked quietly at the woman facing him.

"I don't care if it is, I must do what I think right."

Hester's voice held a dull, parched misery in it. So it meant so much to him, did it? Already too, ten days against ten years. . . .

"Right? . . . Pah!" Hugh shrugged his shoulders, still staring. "It's simply the same thing over again, women simply cannot show mercy towards one of their own sex."

But Hester was already turning, and she stooped to collect her work from the canvas of her deck-chair. She started to walk away from him down the long, deserted deck.

Hugh watched her go, hardness gathering in his eyes.

Very well, then, if that was her game, he would get in first.

But by Gad, he would never forgive her . . . and he swung away, long and lean straight for the purser's cabin.

The purser agreed to say nothing until they reached Port Said as he was afraid of what the captain would say. He also managed to persuade Hester Lane to keep quiet about it, as she also went to him.

"Oh, how long you have been!"

Flame's eyes heavy with sleep, and kept open only by an effort, stared reproachfully over the edge of the white blanket.

"I told you the other day that you were not to keep awake until I came up."

Hugh put a quick hand on the electric switch and flooded the cabin with light.

"I know, but I feel I have to."

Flame's white eyelids dropped and she pressed the backs of her hands against them.

"Why?"

But as Hugh asked the question he felt the derisive nudge of the Devil at his elbow. Yes, he was being a fool; no one knew it better than he, but there it was, he could not help it.

"Why, because I adore seeing you the very, very last thing," sighed Flame. "I adore the sort of heavenly smiling way you say good night. I adore your voice, it's a furry, cuddly voice. I adore the feeling of having you near me . . . simply adore it."

"In fact, I am a very adorable being altogether, evidently," said Hugh, and he came a little nearer to the narrow berth and stared down onto it.

"Perfect," said Flame simply, and she took her hands away from her eyes.

Hugh looked on for a second or two, and then he swung round on his heel.

"Well, I must collect my kit," he said in a voice that he strove to make natural. "Here they are, pyjamas, sponge, toothbrush. Good. Now to put out the light. That's it. Good night!"

"Wait one minute!"

Flame, in the half-darkness, was struggling out from under the coverings.

"Wait one minute. You remember you said once that it wouldn't do for you to kiss me, because the P & O people might find out. Well, but I was thinking, supposing I were to kiss you. That couldn't matter. Besides, no one could know or see.

"Put down your things just for one minute and let me. It might help to stop this *awful* feeling that's always going on inside me. You don't *know* what it is."

Flame crouched back on her heels and began to cry.

"What sort of feeling?"

"Why, the feeling that I want you, want you, *want you!* Want you to have some sort of a feeling for me.

"You don't look at me at all," she sobbed, "and if you do just happen to, because you've got to, it's a sort of stony look, a sort of freezing look. . . ."

"And how do you want me to look?" Hugh had thrust his shaking hands deep down into his pockets.

"As if you liked me a little," Flame cried.

She fell forward on her knees and gathered the blanket up to her face with fingers that were damp and clutching.

There was a long silence. Hugh stood with his dark, well-brushed head a little bent.

Suddenly Flame caught at his hand, and held it to her lips.

"Here, steady on."

Hugh spoke after a palpitating silence.

"Let me go, Flame—you must—I don't want to unfasten your fingers, it seems so . . . Darling . . ."

Then Hugh cursed himself for something worse than a fool as his hand fell free.

"You've said it!" Flame's voice came out on a sobbing breath. "Oh, you've said it, what I always imagined you saying, and what I've died and perished to hear you say."

Flame struggled back into a sitting position, dragged the blankets up round her neck, and flung herself down on her face.

Hugh still remained standing. His pulses were racing and his mind was awhirl. This child his for the taking. This child, inexpressibly dear to him.

Even Hester Lane had been able to see that.

Then the face of his wife, bloated and sodden, floating into the blackness in front of him. Hugh closed his eyes swiftly.

"I've made you angry." Flame had turned over again.

"No, no, you haven't." Hugh had the backs of his hands to his eyes. "No, no, you haven't, don't think that . . ."

"Say 'darling' again!"

"No, I can't," and Hugh's voice was the voice of a boy in distress.

"Why, why can't you?" Flame was sitting up.

"Because I can't, and that's all it's good for you to know."

Hugh had got his self-control back again, and Flame could not see the lines round his mouth, left there by the almost superhuman struggle.

"Besides, it's time you were asleep, it's nearly one o'clock."

"How can I sleep when you go away with things only said in halves?" sobbed Flame, stretching out fiercely anguished hands. "It's not fair . . . it's not fair. You said 'darling,' you ought to go on."

"Go on what?"

As Hugh took a step nearer to the berth, the Devil, who had been sitting with hunched shoulders disgustedly listening, pricked up his pointed ears again.

This man was putting up too good a fight for his liking; however, this sounded more hopeful.

"Just one *weeny* kiss," pleaded Flame, trembling with the fierceness of her longing.

"I'm not good at weeny kisses," Hugh said, standing very still.

"Well, I don't mind what sort of a kiss it is as long as it is a kiss," Flame answered, wondering why her heart was thundering in her ears.

"Very well then; you've asked for it, and you must put up with the consequences. Get out of bed and stand just in front of me. . . ."

Hugh spoke with a catch in his throat.

"On your feet may I stand?" Flame was agitatedly buttoning up the top button of her pyjama coat.

"If you like," and Hugh forced himself to stand rigid while her arms stole round the stiff white collar.

"Now then," and Hugh suddenly laughed quietly aloud.

This child, his entirely to break into love as he wished. His utterly, the droop of Flame's little figure told him that.

Gone, blotted out, the hideous sordid years of the past. He stooped his head.

Flame was speaking:

"When you hold me like this, I sort of see you like I did in Westminster Abbey," she said. "Don't you know even though it's dark I can see your darling angel mouth.

"And even though I'm just a little afraid, don't you know, I'm hardly dressed to be held very tight, yet there's a sort of heavenly joy in being afraid with you. Because you're so good . . . so heavenly, heavenly good."

Flame lifted her face.

The red glow at the back of Hugh's eyes died down abruptly.

"Out of the mouths of babes,"—he let go of her very gently.

"You think too well of me, darling," he said.

As he spoke there was a something in his voice that had not been there before. Flame heard it and trembled.

"Don't let go of me," she breathed.

"Only just for a minute; and not let go, only take hold of you rather differently." Hugh still had his arm round the slender shoulders.

"But what about the kissing?" Flame's trembling voice had tears in it.

"I'll explain about that. Now, look, let go of me just for a minute while I sit down on my berth. That's it. Now come and get on my knee like a nice little girl, and we'll talk quietly."

"But it's suddenly all altered . . . and what about the kissing?" Flame's voice dragged.

The blessed relief of humour came to Hugh's rescue, and he laughed noiselessly.

Flame was not going to let her kiss go without a struggle, evidently! He wiped the sweat from his forehead with a trembling hand.

"You see," he said after a little pause, "this is all wrong, and it's entirely my fault. I won't explain exactly how it's wrong, I expect you know really, although you are such a baby.

"I'm frightfully to blame, desperately, and I'm deadly ashamed of myself. See?"

Hugh stooped his head and stared down at the little figure lying close up against his coat.

"It's something to do with my having said that you were good," lamented Flame; "why, oh why did I say it?"

Hugh's white teeth gleamed for an instant, and then he went suddenly grave.

"Don't regret it. After all, I like you to think I am good, although I'm not in the least, really. And now, it's bed for you; it's late. Get off my knee and I'll tuck you up as I always do."

"Oh, how soon over! And it was going to be so heavenly!"

Flame slid miserably onto the carpet.

"No, not over, really. Besides, heavenly things that aren't right always end up wrong. Now, then, all serene?"

Hugh tucked in the stray end of blanket with a hand that he forced to be businesslike.

"Oh, you're going!" Flame said, clutching at the lean fingers.

"Yes, of course I am; it's nearly time to get up! Let go of me, darling; I'm very tired."

Hugh's voice came weary and flat.

"Yes, all right, of course I will."

Flame dropped the hand she held with a little stab at her heart. He was unhappy, this man she adored; she was tiring him.

"Good night, darling and most precious."

She breathed the words into the soft folds of her pillow.

"Good night."

Hugh went quickly out of the door, and dragged the curtain across roughly behind him.

Roughly, because the whole of his being was screaming out in protest at the decision he had just come to.

There was no longer any doubt about it in his mind. Flame must be sent home from Port Said.

"Flame!" Mary Ashe's gentle blue eyes stood out from a face absolutely white, and she was breathing heavily.

"Yes, what is it? Don't roar out my name like that, somebody will hear."

Flame turned rather wearily from her contemplation of the distant wavering coastline, rapidly becoming clearer. They were due into Port Said at four o'clock that afternoon, and it was just two.

"They're going to send you home from here." Mary Ashe's lips were trembling.

"How do you know?" Flame stood suddenly stock-still and set her back rigid against the rail.

"I've heard. They're talking down in the dining saloon. Mr Keymer and Dr Lane. It was before lunch I heard it really, only I couldn't get to you to tell you then, because of lunch.

"It's all settled . . . the purser knows, and they are only going to wait until the mail has been delivered, and then send on shore and have you handed over to someone to take care of and then sent home."

"Whose idea is it?" Flame was very pale.

"Dr Lane's, I should think, because she's talking the most. Mr Keymer only says 'Yes' and 'No.' "

"Oh!" and the dreadful sick anguish in Flame's soul receded a little.

It was not *his* idea then.

They were not at Port Said yet; there was still time.

The colour began to steal slowly back to her

lips as her mind began to ferret and scurry under the short hair.

"What will you do?" Mary Ashe's voice was pregnant with anxiety.

"I don't know yet, but I'll think of something."

"I've got Miss Peterson's letters; where is she? I'll get this damned business over."

Hugh Keymer spoke with the irritation of extreme misery.

He loathed the whole of this affair more than he could express.

Apart from his feelings of parting with Flame, feelings that he had stamped down and muzzled so far as he could, he dreaded unspeakably telling her, firstly that she was going to be sent home, and secondly that she had lost her mother.

It was not until the sun had sunk a good way down towards the clear-cut line of white breakers that Hugh began to get really anxious.

Then he went down the stairs two at a time.

A second investigation of his cabin had revealed a half-open but empty steel helmet case, and as he stared at it, his tongue had suddenly dried in his mouth. Two precious hours wasted!

He dragged the curtain outside the purser's cabin unceremoniously aside.

"I say, Miss Peterson has managed to get off this ship, somehow," he said.

"But the officer on watch would have seen her go down the ladder."

"Not if she had changed her clothes, which I believe she has done. Look here, what are we going to do?"

Hugh's voice was sharp with anxiety.

"Mr Keymer, I think you are unduly anxious" —the purser smiled a little—"to my mind the whole thing is now perfectly clear. Miss Peterson disguises herself as a boy and gets on board a ship to Port Said. She gets off at Port Said, a city that we all know to be notorious.

"Her business is here, the oldest profession in the world, Mr Keymer, unless I am very much mistaken. We will lodge information with the police, and leave it at that."

"How dare you, sir!" Hugh Keymer's face was white with rage.

The purser stared quietly.

"We will go up to the bridge and inform the captain, and I think you will find that he will confirm what I say."

The captain was elderly and peppery and on the eve of retirement. Although he held Mr Keymer in esteem, because of his literary reputation, he was furiously angry.

"We will inform the police, and leave it at that," he said.

"You don't mean to say that you are going simply to leave a young girl like that in a place like Port Said?"

Hugh's eyes were incredulous.

"Miss Peterson has long since gone to earth, Mr. Keymer." The captain laughed shortly.

"But there are letters for her, I have them."

"You may have. Women of Miss Peterson's profession are adept at covering their tracks."

"I shall also leave the ship here." Hugh spoke with a world of anger in his voice.

"I would beg of you to do nothing so foolish, Mr Keymer," said the captain.

"Kindly give orders for my baggage to be put on shore."

Hugh Keymer turned and walked to his cabin.

Port Said has rightly been named the foulest city in the world.

But Flame did not know all this, when, shaking with excitement, she landed on the rickety landing-stage.

She pressed half-a-crown into the hand of the evil-looking Egyptian boatman, who only winked in his turn to a filthy Egyptian gharrywallah lounging on the box of a battered pair-horse landau.

"Carriage, miss!" he said, and his red fez was insolently cocked over one eye.

"Oh yes, please," said Flame breathlessly.

She clambered rapidly up the high step, badly hampered by her skirt.

After the neat abbreviation of her disguise it was awful, she thought, depositing the parcel she carried on the opposite seat.

But it had been the only thing to be done to ensure easy escape, to change into her girl's clothes. She had done it without the faintest thought of what was to happen next.

If she stayed on that ship she was going to be sent home, so the only thing was to get off.

And off it she now was, clattering up a wide street with houses on each side of it!

Flame stared about her, vastly entertained. This was fun, and she had twenty pounds in her bag, heaps for things to eat and a hotel. . . .

By tomorrow Mr Keymer and Dr Lane would be so mad with fright at her having gone that they would be only glad when she came back, not fussing about sending her home anymore.

So Flame beamed, and a couple of petty officers on shore from a tramp beamed back, which frightened her.

She dragged her little straw hat lower over her eyes and fumbled nervously with her bag.

They had been driving for about twenty minutes when Flame began to look about her rather more critically.

The evening was closing in and it was chilly.

Flame began to get alarmed, she was so very much alone: she had not seen a white face for ages.

She shouted to the Egyptian on the box.

"What missie want?" He turned without stopping the horses and grinned.

"This can't be the way to a hotel. You must have taken the wrong turning. Go back to where there are shops."

But the man on the box only turned round again.

"Stop at that house with the blue verandah." Flame half stood up and pointed.

Then, as she sat down again, she screamed in a wild paroxysm of terror.

An Egyptian had stepped quietly up into the carriage behind her, and had slid his long brown arm round her waist.

"Let go of me at once." Flame hit out and was struggling. "Coachman, coachman!"

But the coachman did not even turn. He was busily engaged in getting down from the box, and when he had got down he started to lead the horses to the side of the road.

"Come now, miss."

The Egyptian, who was dressed in European

clothes with the exception of his headgear, which was a little red fez, spoke ingratiatingly and in excellent English.

"Get out, I tell you!" Flame shouted. "I'm on my way to a hotel. Get out!"

The Egyptian laughed and lolled easily back in the carriage.

"You have then come considerably out of your way, but wait, I will inquire from the coachman."

He got out and went to the horses' heads.

After a little while he came back and held out a hand for Flame.

"All is well, your hotel will be the third house from the end. I will conduct you to it."

"I would rather go by myself," said Flame.

She gathered up her rather unwieldy parcel and stared over it in an angry fright.

"How much do I pay the coachman? Please tell me that, and then go away."

"The coachman has been paid," said the Egyptian, smiling.

"How can he have been?"

But Flame got out, nevertheless, without waiting for an answer. Perhaps this awful man had paid, she thought, and in that case it was better not to know.

"Good evening," she said.

She began to walk rapidly down the road, staring up at the houses as she went.

She would go into the one where she first saw a white face, she thought; then she could shake off this man, whom she could still hear walking quietly along behind her.

Ah! she almost cried out with relief and joy;

a white face, a woman, staring down at her from the verandah almost above her head.

Not speaking, only staring, seeming to be one with the extraordinary quietness of the road.

"Is this a hotel?" said Flame.

She tipped back her head so that all her white throat showed.

"Yes, it is; come up, dearie."

The woman spoke rapidly, and as she spoke she dodged back, and then there was a rush of something flying through the air.

Flame started as with a volley of oaths behind her the Egyptian flung his hands over his face, and staggered back, spluttering.

"Clear out . . . you!" the woman leant far out over the road and swore.

"You . . ." Mercifully Flame could not hear the retort, delivered in the vernacular.

"Further down for the likes of you." The woman was shaking her fist.

Flame stood shivering with her parcel and bag held close to her, still staring upwards.

"Come up, ducky," the woman said.

"Are you sure it is a hotel?" Flame asked.

She was very near to tears. It was quite dark now; why had she come so far? Mr Keymer would be angry with her if he could see her now.

Where was he? Wondering where she was, perhaps. . . . And at that the tears stole out from underneath the white eyelids.

"I'll send down the boy."

As Flame still stood, a native in white clothes came out of an open door at the side of the house, and taking her parcel from her, made signs that she was to follow him up the stairs.

This all seemed more ordinary, and Flame,

surreptitiously wiping her eyes, followed him with relief.

The stairs were brightly lighted, and there were large mirrors set into the walls. They arrived at a wide landing with curtained doors opening off it.

The boy stood outside one and coughed.

"Show the lady in."

The Lady of the Verandah was lying back in a large velvet deck-chair. Flame flushed up to her eyes, for she had hardly anything on.

On the verandah in the dark it had not showed, but here . . . and with a native servant. But when she turned uneasily, the servant had gone.

"Sit down, dearie."

The lady made a gesture towards another velvet chair.

But Flame stood stiffly erect. There was something all wrong about this, she thought.

"I have just got off one of the ships, and I wanted to go to a hotel. But this isn't the sort of place I meant; please tell me how to get back to where I came from."

"And why did you get off a ship?" asked the Lady of the Verandah.

"It's too long to tell you now," faltered Flame.

"Tell me, dearie; it's very important that I should know all about you."

"I was . . . tired of the ship," faltered Flame.

The Lady of the Verandah made an impatient noise with her mouth.

"Ever been to Port Said before?"

"No, and I would like to go back to my ship."

"Which is your ship?"

"The *Akola*."

"Well, you can't go back to her as she was sailing at seven," said the Lady of the Verandah.

"Sailing at seven . . . why, what is the time now, then?" said Flame, suddenly white to the lips.

"Five minutes past."

"But, but . . . how do you know she was sailing then?" stammered Flame, staring round wildly.

"Oh, well, I just happen to know," said the Lady of the Verandah, and she cast rather a curious glance at Flame.

"Anyhow, sit down now; you've got all evening in front of you. I'll be back in half a minute."

The Lady of the Verandah walked to the curtain, brushed it aside, and vanished.

She was back again before Flame had had time to do more than stand and stare with a heart that felt as if it would burst with misery and terror.

The *Akola* gone . . . then Mr Keymer had gone.

All her clothes had gone, everything but the nightdress and brush and comb and washing things that she had in the brown-paper parcel with her.

She was utterly alone in a strange country. The tears began to stream down her face.

"Don't give it up, ducky." The Lady of the Verandah was back again. "Thank your blooming stars you happened to blow in here, and not a few doors lower down."

She raised her head as the native servant, with a subdued cough, drew the curtain aside. Underneath the curtain Flame saw white shoes and the ends of white duck trousers.

"Tell him I'm engaged," said the Lady of the Verandah, scowling.

The curtain fell again, and there was a prolonged colloquy. Then the curtain was drawn aside again and the servant came in.

"Half a minute, duckie."

The Lady of the Verandah went out and did not come back for about ten minutes.

When she did come back her face was very red, and her hands were trembling.

"You little devil, you've set the police on the house! I'll tear your guts out!"

"What do you mean?" Flame was terrified.

"What I say; there's a police officer here, asking for you. And me as rescued you from the dirty scum down below. I'll make you suffer for it, you little bitch, you," and the Lady of the Verandah turned a deep purple.

"But I swear I didn't; policemen are the one people I am afraid of," sobbed Flame, wild with fright and terror.

That was what Nigel had said: policemen meant prison or a reformatory.

"Stop him from coming in somehow, I beseech you to."

The Lady of the Verandah was mollified and partially convinced, and she darted to a chair.

"Sit down there," she hissed, "and drop that old parcel of yours. Pull up your skirt a bit, and shove your hat over your eyes. And when he asks what you are doing here, say I'm your aunt."

She gave a long low whistle.

The tall Egyptian policeman, who had been directed to the house by another Egyptian, with a dripping fez and distorted angry face, came in humming.

He glanced from the Lady of the Verandah to Flame, and then walked up to her with an open notebook in his hand.

"Your name," he said in a foreign accent.

"Mary Jones."

Presumably terror and a certain sense of the dramatic came to Flame's rescue in this first really serious adventure, and she looked up with her head a little on one side.

"Where have you come from?"

"Cairo."

"H'm." The police sergeant was scribbling.

"This lady any relation of yours?"

"Yes, my aunt," said Flame.

She suddenly turned white with the thought of the awful untruths she was telling.

"H'm. She's a pretty little thing!"

The sergeant had put away his notebook and had gone a little nearer to the Lady of the Verandah.

"May I drop in later?" he added with a meaning glance into the heavily lashed eyes.

"Do so, and I'll be here." The Lady of the Verandah burst into laughter indescribably coarse.

She wriggled herself out of her chair, and walked with the tall sergeant to the door.

As the curtain fell behind him, she turned and walked back to her own chair, sat down in it again, and dropped her head in her hands.

"That's torn it," she said, after a prolonged pause, staring across at Flame.

"Why? What!"

"Why, he's coming back; you must clear. Get your parcel and put on your hat. Half a second to let him turn the corner. Now then . . ."

They went quickly down the stairs together.

"What did it all mean?" She tried to ask.

"Oh, shut up, this is serious, this is."

The Lady of the Verandah was in no mood for explanations.,

She jerked her chin at the native servant squatting on his haunches at the foot of the stairs and spoke in some foreign language.

He settled the turban on his head and darted out.

In a minute or two he was back, standing on the iron step of a taxi.

"L'Hôtel de Palais Marine," the Lady of the Verandah spoke in French to the olive-coloured man at the wheel.

Then she added something under her breath that Flame could not hear.

"But where am I going to now?"

Flame, breathless at the rapid march of events, was more bewildered than ever.

First this strange boarding-house place, and now despatched to somewhere else.

"Where is this place that you told the taxi man?" she asked, turning on the step to ask the question.

"Oh, get in and keep quiet."

The Lady of the Verandah was turning her head to look up and down the street.

"Got your parcel? That's it. Ta-ta, then."

Flame suddenly realized that she was thirsty and ravenously hungry into the bargain. Would there be food at this hotel she was going to? Probably.

But a hotel alone, how could she bear it? And alone for weeks or even months, because the *Akola*, with all the people she knew on board, had gone on.

People she knew! Why, that wasn't it at all.

There was only one person she wanted, and by her own mad act she had cut herself off from him for ever.

The taxi turned into a wide gate and slid along a smooth drive edged with shrubs, and began to slacken before drawing up at a wide door out of which bright light was pouring.

Flame cast herself back into the corner of the taxi and flung her hands over her face.

Chapter
Six

Hugh was standing in the hall of the Marine Palace Hotel staring at the Reuter's telegrams as Flame's taxi drew up.

Since five o'clock he had been pacing up and down the hall.

He had left the ship with Flame's luggage and his own at half-past four, and had driven straight to the Marine Palace Hotel. She would be there, he thought, but she was not.

"No sign of any young lady answering to that description," the polite man in the office had said regretfully.

But perhaps Mademoiselle would arrive shortly. Would Monsieur not be wise to engage rooms in readiness?

Hugh had engaged them; it seemed to dull the torment of anxiety a little to feel that these hotel officials thought that Flame was coming.

Very soon he would have to go to the police, he knew, and to the British Consul. But he would give it a little longer first.

Just as he had come to the conclusion that he

could put it off no longer, he heard the swish of tyres on gravel and turned to meet Flame's eyes.

"Oh!" The brown-paper parcel fell to the ground.

"All right, I'll pay the taxi." Hugh came quietly down the steps. "Oh, my God, where have you been?"

His face went white with relief from almost unbearable anxiety.

"Oh, I've been miles," said Flame, and her face too was white, only with rapture.

"Well! Yes, that's all right." Hugh nodded pleasantly as the taxi man touched his hat gratefully. "Well, come along in."

He spoke carelessly; a group of hotel servants were watching them.

"You'll be glad to go to your room and have a wash and change."

As the hotel official in his red fez came forward bowing and rubbing his hands, "Show Madame to her room," he said.

"I haven't anything to change into." Flame spoke in an agitated whisper, staring upwards.

"Lost your luggage? Careless, careless!" Hugh smiled in response to the official's rapidly averted but sympathetic glance.

"Well, we'll soon put that right. Come along upstairs first, anyhow."

Hugh was passionately anxious to get Flame out of the way before she gave the whole thing more hopelessly away.

But the polite official had already strolled back to the office well satisfied. Here was one of those delightful little Port Said idylls that meant so much excellent profit to the hotel.

Above, Hugh and Flame walked along the

wide matted corridor side by side. Flame's heart
was beating in great throbs in her throat.

He was here, beside her, all by himself. The
ship had gone, carrying with it all the people who
got in the way and interfered.

The servant had opened one door and was
walking along to the next. He left both open, sa-
laamed, and withdrew.

Flame went in, and Hugh followed her and
shut the doors.

The two rooms joined one another, then.

Oh, heavenly bliss!

Flame caught her breath, and then suddenly
trembling with a strange shyness, began to fum-
ble with her parcel.

"How dared you try to run away from me?"

Hugh had walked across the floor, and was
standing tall and lean, looking down on the little
figure in front of him.

"Did you mind?" Flame's eyes, upturned,
were wide with joy.

"Mind? Yes, of course I minded." Hugh
caught his lower lip between his teeth. "Tell me why
you did it."

"Because I found out that you and Dr. Lane
had settled to send me home from here. Mary Ashe
told me. I don't want to go home, I want to be with
you always."

"How did Mary Ashe find out?"

Hugh was frowning a little, although far away
in some remote part of him something had begun
to sing.

"She heard you and Dr Lane talking about it
in the dining saloon."

"Oh, I see! And how did you get off the ship
without being seen?"

"I dressed up in my girl's clothes again. No one thought of stopping me. Don't be angry with me."

"No, I'm not angry. But . . ." Hugh smiled. "Did you ever think that if the ship had sailed with me still on her, you would have been very much farther away from me than if you had just gone quietly back to England?"

"No, I never thought of anything except that I didn't want to go away from you," faltered Flame, hanging her head.

"Well!" Hugh took a long breath. "Go, and take off your hat, and then come back to me. There's a great deal I want to hear yet—where you have been since you left the ship, for instance."

Back in his own room, Hugh set his back against the communicating door and shut it with a quick shove. Now, could he trust himself to play the game or could he not?

He had with him Flame's mail, two letters and a cable.

The cable was to announce the death of her mother; he felt pretty certain of that.

He walked out onto the verandah.

If Flame knew that her mother were dead, she would probably not in the least mind going home again. Hugh put his two elbows onto the green iron railing of the verandah and dropped his head in his hands.

Could he, or could he not, risk the chance of losing all this new wonderful happiness at one fell swoop? No, he could not, he came to the conclusion swiftly, raising his head and staring out at the sea.

"I'm ready!" Flame had come quietly up behind him. "Oh, doesn't it look glorious!"

"Yes, it's nice, isn't it? We'll have dinner out here in a few minutes. You must be ravenously hungry, but tell me first about what you have been doing since you left the ship."

"Well, it was like this. . . ."

Flame told the whole story, looking like a frightened child in her soft grey dress with the frill round the neck.

"What sort of a place do you think it can have been?" she ended up shyly.

"I can't conceive," said Hugh, speaking rather shortly and huskily. "Anyhow, I'll find out tomorrow. I should like to thank that woman for looking after you."

What reward could he give that would be adequate? That woman, probably sunk in depths of vice beyond imagination, and yet with enough of the Divine still left in her to spare the child who had stumbled unawares on the threshold of hell.

He felt the tears burn behind his eyelids.

Dinner was over.

Gaston, the French headwaiter, appeared twice during this wonderful meal, firstly to inquire what Monsieur and Madame would drink, and lastly to bring the exquisitely made Turkish coffee.

"He thinks I'm your wife . . . he calls me 'Madame.' "

Flame, who had been dreadfully hungry before, was now in the wildest spirits.

"Does he?"

Hugh closed his eyes abruptly as a vision of the woman who bore his name fled across him.

"How would you like to be?" he asked abruptly, opening his eyes again.

"But you have one."

"Yes, I know, but supposing I hadn't."

"Well, I should love it," said Flame, speaking rather breathlessly.

Why did her heart suddenly begin to beat so madly? she wondered.

Hugh suddenly got up and walked to the rail of the verandah.

"Give her those letters and cable," his conscience was screaming out the words as his eyes, rather haggard, rested on the divine panorama spread out in front of him.

He turned round abruptly.

"I've got some letters and a cable for you," he said, and his voice was quick and hard.

"Have you? Well then, I don't want them."

Flame's response was instant, and she half got up out of her chair.

"Don't get them," she cried, and she flung out her hands.

"Why not?" Hugh turned from the door into his room.

"Mother will say I'm to go back."

Hugh caught his breath. That that cable contained the news of that mother's death, he had not the faintest doubt. And that that would alter the whole of this child's outlook on life he had not the faintest doubt either.

"You'd better have them," he said hoarsely.

"No, no; I tell you I don't want them!" Flame had begun to cry. "It's because you want to get rid of me, I know it is."

"Flame! Look here, stop crying and listen to me. How can you stay with me? Tell me now! Come onto my knee, you silly little child, and tell me."

But in spite of his bantering words Hugh's

breath was coming heavily as he dropped into a low wicker chair and held out his arms.

"Oh, you've got that heavenly smoky, manly smell in your neck . . . I adore it!"

Flame had flung back her head and was squashing her face into the brown throat.

"Oh, what a blissful evening this is being!"

"Look here, stop for a minute."

With almost superhuman self-control Hugh put his hand under Flame's head and drew it away from him a little.

"You're shaking all over," said Flame curiously.

"Am I?" Hugh laughed shortly.

Then he suddenly let her slip quietly off his knee.

"Look here, you have no conception what you are doing," he said roughly, and his eyes had a dreadful look in their depths. "Go to bed, before it is too late."

"Too late for what?"

"For me to remember . . ." And then Hugh stopped.

Flame's face lifted like a little flower. And that other face, red-veined and swollen, smiling stupidly.

"Remember what?"

"Nothing." Hugh laughed rather wildly.

"I don't want to remember anything except that I adore you," said Flame, smiling tremulously.

"Ah . . ." And then Hugh flung conscience, honour, everything to the winds.

This child loved him, and here they were miles away from everyone. She was his, this little sweet thing; his, every atom of her.

He stooped and gathered her up to his heart.

"Now are you going to kiss me?" asked Flame.

"Yes, I am," said Hugh, and he lifted her from the floor.

"Oh, kissing is the most heavenly thing!"

Flame drew a long breath and lifted her arms slowly above her head.

"But I couldn't bear it from anyone but you."

"No, that's as it should be," said Hugh as he gathered the little figure rather closer to him.

"It makes me feel all sort of seethy and mad inside."

"Does it?" Hugh asked. His eyes were fixed on a moth blundering up and down the globe of the electric light.

"Yes, frightfully mad inside," said Flame, and she stirred a little uncomfortably. "Will it go off?"

"Probably," Hugh answered quietly.

"Oh! In a way, I like it," said Flame shyly.

"Do you? Well, I'm glad," said Hugh. "But it's time for little girls to go to bed."

She was his, so he could afford to wait. Also she was a child, and a child must be led tenderly and sympathetically—into the wilderness of love.

Flame, blinking long eyelashes, stared bewildered for a moment or two.

Where was she? No white tiny cabin and serge curtain blowing in the doorway, but a wide, sun-filled room, and a tall figure in striped pyjamas standing by her bed.

"Oh!" and she burrowed, suddenly shy, under the sheet.

"Come along out, your tea will get cold!" Hugh was laughing like a boy.

Every twinge of conscience gone, he had slept dreamlessly and waked with a wild feeling of exhilaration.

"I must brush my teeth first." Flame was looking out again, the sheet held close up under her chin.

"All right!"

Hugh turned and swung away. Flame, watching him go, with her heart in her eyes, trembled.

Even to *see* him gave her the wildest, maddest thrill of rapture all over her; what when he kissed her again, which he probably would when she had washed and brushed her hair and put on her dressing-gown?

"There you are!" Hugh turned at the soft footfall. "Come and look out, did you ever see anything lovelier?"

He flung out a quiet arm and drew her close to his side.

"Did you sleep well?" He looked down at her.

"Yes, very." Flame's heart was beating very hard.

Now for the kiss!

Hugh was smiling, and he held out his arms.

Flame was in them, clinging desperately.

"I thought you weren't going to," she breathed.

"Did you? Well, you were mistaken. Beloved, dearest little thing; oh, you, *you* . . ."

Hugh laid his mouth on each soft shut eye in turn.

"You what?" Flame was quivering with joy.

"You joy of my soul." Hugh set her down gently. "Now, that's enough for this hour of the morning, this is the time for *chota hazeri*. You sit over there and pour out, and I'll sit here and see how badly you did it."

"How do you know I shall do it badly?"

"You're sure to, because you're so young. No, that's not so bad," as Flame's small hands moved deftly among the flowered china. "Quite good. Now I'll butter the toast, one piece for each of us and a plantain each, too. Don't speak with your mouth full, it's bad manners."

"I wasn't going to!" Flame spoke indignantly.

Hugh flung back his head and laughed tumultuously. Then he went suddenly grave.

"Oh, God, I'm so happy I can't help making a fool of myself!" he said, and he got up and walked round the table.

"Is it because you've got me you're so happy?" said Flame, catching one of the lean brown hands in hers and holding it to her face.

"Yes, it is. Tell me you're happy too, and then I shall be happier still."

Hugh was standing, one hand on the cropped head, staring out to sea.

"I'm so happy that I feel I shall die with happiness. I'm so happy that I feel absolutely mad with happiness. Oh, Hugh! Take me in your arms, or else I *can't* believe it."

Flame suddenly dropped the brown hand she was holding and burst out crying.

"Darling!"

In a second she was in his arms, held passionately close.

"Darling, what is it? Not tears at this hour of the morning! Come, cheer up! What's it all about?"

Hugh held her a little way away from him,

and then drew her close again, pressing her head against his heart.

But he stared over her head with eyes that were tender and exultant at the same time.

Flame was taking it hard, the passionate little mouth had not lied. Ah! But he would be good to her, he would. She had nothing to fear, with him.

"Better?" He spoke tenderly.

"Yes, thank you." Flame was wiping her eyes rather tremulously.

"I don't know why I suddenly go off like that. I think it is because I get a sort of mad feeling inside, and I don't know what to do with it."

"Probably."

But Hugh's eyes were fixed on the straight blue line of the horizon. Suddenly his conscience took him by the throat.

"You hound! You know perfectly well that if you are ever to know an instant's happiness in the future you *must* show her those letters and cable, now, this instant."

He swung round and walked quickly into his room to get them.

"Why must I read them now?" Flame was holding them in her hand.

"Because I want you to. There are only two and the cable. Read the cable first."

Hugh's heart was beating heavily in his throat, and he felt a little sick.

"All right." Flame tore the white Eastern Telegraph envelope across. " '*Something has happened; wait till you get my letter at Colaba. Nigel.*' Oh, whatever can it be?"

"Read the letters." Hugh's hands were in his pockets. Reprieve!

"They're only quite short."

Flame's eyes were running down the small, neat writing.

"Gerald says, *'Be good, and go straight to Waterton's daughter at Colaba,'* and I shall be all right. And Nigel says . . ."

Flame tore the envelope across.

"Nigel says that Waterton writes to say that Mincemeat had hysterics when she found we had gone, but that when Waterton explained, she was all right, and she went to spend the rest of the day with a friend, and Waterton let her have the Rolls to keep her quiet."

"And who is Mincemeat?" Hugh was leaning back, looking across the small space that separated them.

"My governess."

Flame was replacing the letters in their envelopes.

"I wonder what the thing is that Nigel wants to tell me," she ruminated thoughtfully.

"What do you think it could be?"

"Something about Falaise." Flame suddenly looked up. "Oh! if only I could be there with you."

"Why?"

"Because Falaise sort of gets into my soul, like you do," said Flame. "Like when you come close to me and put your arms round me. It warms me all through and through."

"Come here," he said.

"What, have I said something to make you angry?"

Flame stood up abruptly, letting the letters on her lap slip on to the floor.

"No, not angry. Look here."

Hugh had his hands on the soft shoulders below him.

"Supposing your being with me meant that you could never see Falaise again, would you think it was worth it?"

"Could it mean that?"

"Quite easily."

"That I couldn't see Nigel either?"

"Yes, possibly not Nigel either."

Flame stood still for a minute.

"But why should it?"

"Because, darling, a man of my age and a child of your age are not supposed to go about together. Oh, how ridiculous that sounds! Flame, it is so difficult to explain to you. Look here, I must try and make it clearer."

Hugh sank his head into his hands.

"Wait a minute. Will you always want me with you?" Flame interrupted eagerly.

"Always." Hugh's voice was muffled.

"Shall we be able to go where people won't interfere?"

"Yes."

"Well, then, I don't care about *anything* but you, I don't want *anyone* but you. I only want to be where I can see your darling, *darling* mouth, so heavenly and understanding, and feel your precious, *precious* arms round me."

She gave a heartbroken cry.

"Hugh, I love you, I love you! Don't send me away from you!"

Flame was weeping wildly.

"Ah! But I ought not to, I ought not to!" Hugh's conscience was suddenly desperately awake.

This child, innocent almost beyond imagina-

tion, clinging to him in purest love and trust, what
was he going to do to her? Supposing she turned
and bitterly reproached him afterwards?

"No, look here, I must think. . . ."

He tried to unfasten the clinging fingers.

"You'll kill me. I tell you, if you send me
home I shall throw myself overboard."

Flame took a couple of steps backward.

"You're tired of me, that's what it is; you
think I shall be a bother when you want to write."

The soft mouth was set suddenly in a hard
line.

"Be quiet. I don't think anything of the
kind." Hugh was breathing heavily.

"Well, what is it, then? There must be something. Last night you loved me and kissed me; today you only keep on thinking of things that might
make you want to send me away from you."

Her eyes sought his.

"Hugh, don't you love me? Tell me, has anything come to make you not love me? Tell me, I
must know. . . ."

"My God no. No, it's only that—Flame, you
don't in the least understand what it means. And I
feel now that perhaps I'm taking advantage of you,
a cowardly advantage that I shall regret for the
rest of my life. Perhaps one day you will reproach
me, and that would absolutely finish me."

Hugh's face suddenly went pale and old.

"But I love you." Flame came quietly nearer.

"Yes, I know you do now, but perhaps when
you find out . . ."

Hugh stopped abruptly and took the little upturned face between his hands.

"Find out what?"

"Well—nothing."

Hugh took a long breath. No, this settled it. It was too much to expect from any man.

He stooped and lifted the little figure in his arms.

"All that awful misery for nothing," whispered Flame, drying her eyes on the lapel of the striped coat.

"Yes, but it had to be. Now then, wipe your dearest face on my hanky and let's start *chota hazeri* all over again. You sit on my knee, and then I can see that you don't fill your mouth too full."

"Oh, Hugh!" Flame drew a long sobbing breath.

Hugh stooped and buried his mouth in the little white throat turned up to him.

"Beloved!"

A very perfect day was very near to its close.

Hugh had taken her shopping, and she had spent nearly all her twenty pounds on clothes. Hugh said he would look after her when all her money had been spent.

So the morning had been a perfect success, and back again at the hotel, lunch had been served in a beautiful little private sitting-room adjoining Flame's bedroom. Then there had been a long, dreamless sleep on the big chesterfield sofa covered with grey linen.

Hugh had insisted on that.

Almost after tea Hugh had gone out, not saying where he was going, but only laying his hand gently on her head and saying that he would not be away for long. He had returned just in time for dinner.

That evening Hugh entered her bedroom, very tall and lean in striped pyjamas.

"Ready?" he said, standing in the door giving on to the verandah.

He looked quite black against the silvery pathway to the moon, and he stood with his hands in his pockets.

"Oh, I say, I'm not in bed!" Flame faltered a little and shrank back against the wall.

"Never mind. What does it matter? You're quite dressed. Come over here!"

Hugh leant back against the wall and held out his arms.

"No." Flame took hold of both her ears like a frightened child.

"But I say yes! Come here."

Flame dared not disobey, but she went laggingly and with her chin on her neck. He was different, there was no doubt about it.

Just as heavenly, Flame felt the same little soft thrill run over her as he spoke, but without the sort of tender heavenliness that made his arms a shelter.

"Now then, say you're sorry for keeping me waiting."

Hugh put a hand on each side of the soft face and drew Flame close to him.

"I am very, very sorry." Flame's breast was heaving.

"Oh . . ." She caught her breath suddenly.

"What's the matter?"

"Why, it's the feeling of not having very much on. . . ."

Flame caught hold of the lean fingers.

"What's the matter?"

"Nothing really . . . only . . ." Flame's colour was coming and going swiftly.

"Why—what is it?"

Hugh spoke caressingly, although there was something in his eyes that was not caressing.

"I don't know . . . only I feel somehow as if I . . . *Hugh!* No, don't . . . no, don't!"

Flame suddenly stood still and wrung her hands.

"Don't what? I thought you liked me to hold you so close?" Hugh laughed, a funny laugh in which there was no mirth.

"Yes, but I do . . . I do. It's only that . . ."

The rest of the sentence was lost in a strangled cry as Flame was swept up into savage arms.

It was only a very little movement, but it awoke the man who had only just dropped off to sleep.

Conscience keeps her own particular shafts for the very early morning, and Hugh had had his full mead of them since Flame, with little inarticulate murmurings of love, had dropped off to sleep in his arms.

Hers was the sleep of youth, deep and quiescent.

"Beloved, what is it?" He did not move his chin from the little head.

"You did shave again, after all." Flame's small hand was wandering.

"Oh, Flame!"

In the midst of his torment of thought Hugh laughed aloud. The vagaries of a woman's mind, who could follow them?

"Yes, I did," he said. "Why, do you mind?"

"No, I love you because you are so polite in those ways," said Flame.

Then sleepily a fuller consciousness came
back to her and she suddenly shrank away from
him.

Hugh caught in his breath with a dreadful
stab at his heart. "No!" he said, and he drew her
fiercely back to him.

"You'll think less of me now, I know . . .
you'll think less of me!" Flame sobbed wildly.

"I shall not." Hugh's voice died in an awful
despair. Already?

Then common sense came to his aid.

"Beloved and most precious, I shall not," he
said. Very gently he drew the little cowering figure
up from under the sheet. "And if you say that,
Flame, you will kill me—do you hear? You will
kill me."

"Are you sure?"

Flame had struggled up into a sitting position, and Hugh could see her round eyes searching
his through the darkness.

"Absolutely sure." Hugh, up on his elbow,
spoke with clenched hands.

"Oh." Flame sat perfectly still for a minute or
two.

Hugh, with his head dropped in his hands,
sat still too. Flame must fight this out herself; it
was not fair to weaken her defences as he knew he
could weaken them if he liked.

"I still love you most frightfully . . . most
frightfully. In fact, I think I love you much more
now."

Flame spoke in a fierce whisper, heavy with
shame.

"Do you? Thank God for that." Hugh spoke
simply. He raised his head from his hands with a
long, halting sigh.

"And now, shall we go to sleep again?" Flame asked.

She spoke in a voice from which all hint of tragedy had gone, and which only held a sort of childish satisfaction in its tones.

The haggard line of blue between the dark eyelashes suddenly narrowed in laughter. This child! He gathered her closely into his arms.

"Are you sure you wouldn't rather be by yourself?" he said tenderly.

"Oh *no!* I think this is the most blissful part, to be absolutely, absolutely close to you in the dark," breathed Flame.

She leant back and searched the vaguely seen face anxiously.

"That is, if you are sure that you like it too."

Hugh did not reply, and Flame, after a little silence, put out an anxious hand.

"You're shaking all over."

"Am I?"

Flame's wandering hand came in contact with something white and faintly gleaming and she drew back shyly.

"You're laughing at me."

"And if I am, never mind, most precious, and most dear," said Hugh, and he drew the little confiding head back into the hollow of his shoulder again.

It was the next night that he told her, lying out in a long chair on the verandah, the big moon making the yellow hair a puddle of gold against the black dinner-jacket.

"I want to tell you something." Hugh's free hand was gripped damply down by his side.

"What sort of thing?" asked Flame, nestling closer.

"This," said Hugh, and then he told her.

There was a very long silence. Then Flame sat up.

"Then Mother actually isn't there?"

"No."

"Only Waterton and Nigel."

"Yes."

"What did she die of, do you know?" asked Flame, pushing the short hair back from her forehead.

"Something sudden, I gather," said Hugh briefly.

It was not necessary to tell this child the true horror of the thing.

"Oh!" And then there was another long silence.

Flame turned and took the brown face between her hands.

"When did you know, Hughie?" she said, and Hugh could see the rather round eyes searching his.

"I knew about two days out from Marseilles," said Hugh.

In the agony of the confession he let his eyelids drop over his haunted eyes.

"Oh!" And then there was another long silence.

Then Flame, with a little halting sigh, let herself drop back on to the pleated shirt-front. "What a mercy I didn't know before!"

"Why?" asked Hugh, knowing exactly what the answer would be and yet fiercely desirous of hearing his death-warrant spoken aloud.

"Why, because perhaps if I had known I might have felt that I ought to go back," Flame answered simply.

At that Hugh moved his long stretched-out legs.

"Let me get up, darling," he said quietly.

He let Flame slip very gently off his knee, struggled up out of the sagging canvas, and walked in out of the moonlight.

And there, in the darkened sitting-room, Flame found him, after about half an hour's gentle wondering what could have become of him, flung out straight on his face, gripping one rounded end of the grey linen sofa.

"Oh, Hughie, you've got a pain!"

Hugh drew a long halting sigh.

"No," he said, and he rolled over on to his side. "Flame," and Flame trembled at the funny altered voice.

"Flame, tell me that you love me. You are to! I can't stand it! Say that you would have come even if you had known that your mother wasn't there. You are to say it!"

Hugh sat up, and against the pale silvery oblong of the verandah door Flame could see the disordered hair.

"Are you positive that you haven't got a pain?" she asked tremblingly.

This was something so absolutely different in the way of a Hugh. Generally he was so sort of omnipotent; here he was imploring, agonized.

And then Flame's mind leaped to the true solution of the thing.

"Beloved and most precious, I should never have gone back," she said.

With a little loving catch in her voice she dropped down onto the couch beside the seated figure and asked:

"Dearest and most heavenly, how could I

have lived without you? How could I have lived?
Hughie . . . Hughie!"

Flame suddenly began to cry.

"Say it again." Hugh had his mouth pressed
to the wet eyelids.

"I will, I will! I never could have gone,
Hughie! And you say too, that you are glad you've
got me."

Suddenly shaken and terrified with the strange
turn that things were taking, she craved to be re-
assured.

"Glad I've got you!"

Hugh stood up, and there was a funny steely
sound in his voice.

"Glad I've got you? My God! Flame, Flame!"
and Flame was swept to a thundering heart.

"I like it best like this," said Flame, with a
little sobbing satisfied sigh, as out under the stars
again they lay quietly spread out in the deck-
chair.

"Then you shall always have it like this,
Flame," said Hugh, with his mouth on the soft
hair.

"Always exactly what I want?"

"Always so long as it is possible," said Hugh
tenderly, staring out to sea.

"You and Nigel, Falaise and Waterton," said
Flame, feeling round the beloved face with a small
wandering hand.

"If God is good," said Hugh, wondering stupidly how he dared take that sacred Name on
his lips.

"But He is," said Flame reproachfully.

"Then perhaps He will help us," said Hugh,
and his heart cried out: "Oh, God, do . . . do!"

He was on his knees like a supplicating child.

But the Man of Sorrows turned away His face. This man had known better. He could not escape the suffering due to him.

Chapter
Seven

Kashmir, land for lovers! Nature run riot in a beauty that sets your senses athrill. Cornfields starred with poppies, and fringed with purple irises.

Pine forests standing steep and black against the blue sky, and heavenly-clear mountain streams dashing themselves over the stones with a song in their hurrying. Around it all, like a sentinel with drawn sword, the snows, stern and forbidding in their icy purity.

"An emerald in a setting of platinum," Flame exclaimed excitedly when she saw it first.

"Don't you see what I mean?" she asked, as she laid her head gently against her lover's arm standing at the door of their tent.

"Yes, I do, darling."

Hugh drew her to him almost fiercely as he spoke. For the relief to be actually there was so overwhelming.

Since that day nearly four months before when they had been flung into one another's arms at Port Said, he had gone through torments of anxiety.

At first it had been easy, they had wandered into the desert.

"It's like *The Sheik,* hooray!"

Flame had rocked her little body from side to side as she surveyed the encampment of luxurious tents.

"The what?" Hugh had just come in from giving orders about the stabling of the horses, and he held out a tender hand.

"*The Sheek,* you know, that book about the girl that was carried off by someone."

"You mean *The Sheikh!*" Hugh was in convulsions of laughter.

"Oh, is it 'Shake'? I didn't know. *Hugh!* I love you when you laugh like that and show all your heavenly teeth!"

Flame, in her riding-breeches, made a little run and, jumping, curled her legs round her lover's waist like a child.

"Baby, let go of me! Sweet! Are you happy?" Hugh bent his dark head.

"Happy! I can't tell you how happy! In fact, it isn't like being happy at all. It's like something much more. It's like something too much to explain . . . I can't say it!"

Flame drew a long, gasping breath.

So Hugh was content. He was content with a wonderful abiding peace of mind that, under the circumstances, ought not to have been his at all.

But to a man of his temperament every day of his marriage had been a hell, and to emerge from it into this ecstasy of happiness was heaven.

So every day and every night was a rapture,

and they rode together and explored, and Hugh
wrote, and Flame stooped over rolls of muslin and
crêpe de Chine bought in Port Said, and made
ridiculous little frocks and undergarments to re-
plenish her wardrobe.

Both were utterly and completely happy, with
the happiness that generally comes before the blow
that finally shatters it for ever.

This particular blow fell one evening, after
a day on horseback.

Hugh was standing with his glass to his hand
watching the little gassy bubbles wriggling up to
the surface.

The first drink of the day; delicious; he drew a
long breath of content as he tipped back his head.

"Oh! . . ."

It was a funny little swaying sigh that came
from behind him.

"Sleepy, darling?"

Hugh turned, laughing tenderly.

But Flame was a funny little crumpled heap
on the floor behind him.

As he stooped, terrified, to lift her, Hugh's
eyes had a look in them as if they had suddenly
been struck blind.

"No!" It was as if he were screaming defiance
at an unseen enemy as he laid her on the couch.

"No!" Hugh's mind went tearing, hurrying
back frantic into the recesses of memory.

But later, as he knelt beside the little camp-
bed into which he had put Flame with the tender-
ness of a mother, he knew it with a deadly
certainty.

Flame was very shy.

"Put your head very close and I'll whisper,"
he said.

"You ought to have told me that before, be-loved." Hugh's lips were white.

"Why? Why should I? Why does it matter? Besides, you see, I thought perhaps it was because we were in a different sort of country or something, and that perhaps . . ."

But in a very short time did away with any hope of that kind.

When one morning Flame waved away her *chota hazeri,* and sat staring blankly in front of her with her tiny handkerchief pressed to her mouth, Hugh knew that she must be told.

He took her on his knee to tell her.

Flame listened blankly.

"But however do you know?"

Hugh laughed shortly.

"Darling, take it from me that I do know," he said, and he carried the hand that he held to his mouth.

"But can we, when we aren't properly mar-ried?" Flame spoke after a long pause.

Hugh felt dimly that someone was answering for him; answering with brutal frankness.

"No, you can't. But unfortunately for you, you've entrusted yourself to a criminal fool so you can," and as he heard he groaned.

"Do you feel ill too?" Flame was instantly all anxiety.

"No, no!" Hugh pressed the little head back into his shoulder.

"When will it come?" Flame spoke after an-other long pause.

Hugh told her, and then another long silence fell between the two. Flame broke it:

"You know there's something most terrifical-ly rapturous about it. I didn't realize it at first.

Your child! Something that will really belong to you and me like nothing else could. Aren't you glad?"

"Flame?"

As Hugh held her passionately close, staring blindly over her head, one great tear detached itself and ran down his face.

"Where shall I go to have it? Falaise?"

Flame spoke joyfully and ruminatively.

"No, darling, you can't do that."

Then Hugh let her slip gently off his knee, and getting up, he walked away to the door of the tent.

Flame saw the brown hand trembling on the gay silk handkerchief.

"You mind!"

In a flash she was by his side.

"No, no!" Hugh had his lower lip between his teeth.

"You do! Beloved, beloved, you are disappointed or something!"

Flame was clinging to him passionately, staring upward. The darling face was all twisted.

Why, oh why? . . . She scanned it, the tears beginning to form in her own eyes.

Hugh saw the little face through the blur of his own tears, and he made instant resolve that if it killed him Flame should never know what this awful blow was going to mean to them.

It must be kept from her, somehow—the horror of disgrace; the torment of trying to keep it quiet; the terror of running up against people that they knew.

She must be got away, somehow, somewhere! But how? And where? with the present-day fool precautions of passports!

But he only smiled, and blew his nose with a little shaky laugh.

"Sweet, you took me so tremendously by surprise, that's all it is. Of course I am glad. Come along and let us talk it all over."

But later that night, when Flame was asleep, curled up like a little kitten in the bed drawn close to his, Hugh took his writing materials outside and wrote till the small hours of the morning.

The longest letter was a letter to his lawyer; he had already written once to him, but there had not been time to get an answer.

But this time the letter was a little different, and when he read it, the nice lawyer, who had known Hugh for years, had to wipe his spectacles more than once.

"But it's useless," he said, as he went to get the Bradshaw down from the fat bookshelf. "The woman's a devil; I saw that plainly enough the last time I went down."

The second letter was one to Gerald Forsythe. It was a letter that left Hugh's hair a little greyer than it had been when he began it.

But it had to be written; there had been no answer to Flame's first letter to her brother, and she was beginning to wonder.

When Gerald Forsythe got it, he read it twice, and then also got up to take down a Bradshaw, and having with a good deal of grunting located a train, ran for his breakfast, got heavily into a taxi, and made his way to Waterloo.

"You've got to be reasonable about the whole thing, my boy."

Colonel Forsythe stood with his back to the gorgeous wood fire in the old tapestry-hung hall.

Falaise was full of riotous young people,

all out shooting for the moment. On the receipt
of Colonel Forsythe's telegram, Nigel had stayed
at home.

"Reasonable! You ask me to be reasonable
when I am dealing with the man who has seduced
my sister! I tell you I won't listen to his cursed
letter."

Nigel Peterson was white with rage.

"You must, Nigel, this affair has got to be
properly tackled. I hold no brief for Keymer, although here he certainly writes like a broken-
hearted man; Stephens says the same, I saw him
yesterday. But in the face of this new and overwhelming catastrophe something has got to be done.

"Mrs Keymer must be induced to divorce him
somehow; we must try and persuade her. When we
try and persuade her, you must be there too."

"As if the devil couldn't have prevented . . ."
Nigel was fingering a paperweight with a trembling
hand.

"Quite so!" Colonel Forsythe shrugged his
shoulders a little. "Quite so, Nigel. But it's easy
to say that now. The point now is, that something
has got to be done. The time is past for harking
back to what might or might not have been."

Although large, India can be found to be a
very small place, as many people have often ex-
perienced to their cost, and Hester Lane was only
vaguely dismayed when one day Jeewan brought
her a card on a tray.

"She would be here!" Hester dropped the card
with a little groan. "All right, Jeewan; give the
Memsahib my salaams and tell her that I will be
there in one moment."

Mrs Holroyd-Browne; Hester had heard vague

mention of the advent of a new regiment. But that it should be just this one woman of all others who should be the wife of the arriving Colonel!

Hester groaned as she slipped a flowered cotton-voile frock off a hanger and carefully got herself into it.

"My dear . . . after all these months," Mrs Holroyd-Browne was fluttery and effusive. "And really . . . I should hardly have known!"

She held both Hester's hands at arm's length.

"Oh, I don't know . . . India always suits me very well." Hester's eyes wavered and fell.

"Yes, but for the last ten days on that dreadful voyage. My dear, will you ever forget it? And you . . . such an intimate friend of that poor dear Mr Keymer . . . as we all said at the time, it was *awful* for you! . . ."

Mrs Holroyd-Browne was watching Hester's face like a lynx.

"Do sit down, won't you?" Hester very gently detached her hands. "And you'll have tea? Yes, do; I assure you it isn't the faintest trouble; only one moment . . ."

Hester walked swiftly out of the room.

"Tea will be here in just a moment"—she smiled when she returned—"and fortunately, both my colleagues happen to be at home, too, as it is a half-holiday. So we shall be a pleasant little party. A visitor from Cantonments is always a treat to us."

"Really . . ." Mrs Holroyd-Browne was wondering how to begin.

She would have to be quick, because apparently the party *à deux* was not to come off; two more of these dull women would shortly appear on the scene.

But the change in this dull one really was re-markable, and Mrs Holroyd-Browne's eyes dwelt anew on the muslin frock, obviously not a local production. But wasn't there some talk of a man ...some famous doctor staying at the Civil and Military Hotel? Anyhow ... and Mrs Holroyd-Browne leant forward.

"My dear," she said, "I knew you would be interested, and as a matter of fact I think you real-ly ought to know it. I have just come back from Kashmir, where I have been spending the hot weather. While I was at Gulmerg I met one of those very nice young men who came out with us.

"Well, he had been up into the wilds after bear, and one evening, just as he was pitching his camp, who should pass but that dreadful girl, dressed *as* a girl this time, by the way. He knew her at once, by her extraordinary black eyebrows and eyelashes. Also, she was accompanied by a man that we both know. ..."

Mrs Holroyd-Browne laughed meaningly.

"Really!" Hester's voice came dumb and faint to her ears.

"Yes." Mrs Holroyd-Browne spoke more sharply this time.

This woman was a fool to try and dissemble, when her infatuation had been so pitifully obvious.

"Yes. But of course the terrible part is yet to come. I know Mr Mason very well," Mrs Holroyd-Browne simpered, "or he would never have told me what he did. But he said that it was only too obvious what ..."

Mrs Holroyd-Browne broke off, satisfied this time.

"*No!*" and through her misery Hester's soul screamed denial to this anguish.

Not Hugh, Hugh! Not Hugh, knowing the tragedy that it would mean.

"Yes, really! But under the circumstances . . . and Mr Keymer being, as he is, a man of the world, wouldn't you have thought. . . . ?"

Mrs Holroyd-Browne became very involved and obscure.

Mercifully for Hester, at this moment Hilly and Miss Harris came in. So the rest of the visit passed in a sort of horrid detached nightmare.

Mrs Holroyd-Browne had to leave without any further allusion to the matter that was occupying her thoughts to the exclusion of everything else.

Left alone, Hester pushed the hair stupidly out of her eyes. Hugh and Flame Peterson in Kashmir, within touch of her, really.

Flame shortly to become a mother . . . no, no, *no!*

Hester rose and began to pace up and down the room.

The Larches stood some way back from the road in a very nice garden. The road was a very respectable one, wide and shady, situated in one of the wealthiest suburbs in south-west London.

The long Rolls-Royce that stopped outside the gate looked quite in keeping with the whole thing, as did the three men who got out of it, and the young chauffeur who stood attentively holding the door open.

"Oh, my God, how I loathe this!"

Sir Nigel spoke with the exasperated agony of youth on the rack, as they walked together up the beautifully kept drive.

"Never mind, old chap; it won't last long."

Colonel Forsythe spoke kindly, laying an unob-
trusive hand on the young arm close to his.

"But it's so . . ."

Then Nigel Peterson caught in his breath as
the front door came into view.

Such a fine front door, with plate-glass windows let into each side of it, showing a wide hall
full of beautiful chrysanthemums in full bloom.

A trim maid answered the door; no ordinary
apron and cap here, but a dress of softest black
cashmere, and a wide, flat bow on the neat hair
behind.

"Yes, step this way, will you, please, sir?" The
trim maid spoke to Mr Stephens, whom she already knew by sight.

"Thank you."

She led them all, single file, behind her into
the drawing-room.

At first Nigel thought it was empty; then he
caught his breath as a woman rose from a chair
drawn up close to a writing-table.

But it was the Matron of the Home, whom
Mr Stephens knew, and very much liked.

"How do you do?"

She had a low, pleasant voice, and she held
out a hand with several very nice rings on it. She
held Nigel's hand a little longer than the others.

She had heard of the sad catastrophe that had
befallen the House of which this boy was the head,
and she pitied him from the bottom of her heart.

But she also knew Mrs Keymer, so her sympathy was not quite so unmixed with other emo-
tions as it ought to have been.

Nigel could only stare round with tormented
eyes. Was that other woman perhaps lurking
about here?

The other woman before whom he would have to stand shamed and humiliated as the brother of the girl who had stolen away her husband.

He breathed in the dusky wintry scent of the chrysanthemums with nostrils that were twitching.

"I will send for Mrs Keymer. But I think I ought to tell you . . ."

Then the gentle voice dropped and with an upward glance at Mr Stephens she walked a little away, the lawyer following her.

While they talked, Nigel and Colonel Forsythe stood together close to the fireplace, in which a bright fire was burning. It was a beautiful, chilly September day.

Nigel thought resentfully of the shooting he was missing. Then something stirred at his feet, and Nigel saw a tiny pink tongue and stretching extended paws.

"Oh, you pet!" He lifted the smoke-grey kitten and held it to his face.

As Mrs Unwin saw him like that she stopped wondering how Hugh Keymer could have done the thing that he had done. Brother and sister were exactly alike, so Mr Stephens had told her.

"I will get Mrs Keymer to come down," she said, and she walked to the door, shutting it carefully behind her.

Left alone, the three men did not speak. Mr Stephens had taken a small pocket diary out of his pocket and was scribbling in it.

Colonel Forsythe had one hand curled round his carefully concealed pipe, wishing to God he could smoke it.

Nigel was trembling and feeling a little sick. He had put the kitten back on the rug again.

Then the door opened and shut, and as it shut

there was a gleam of something white from out-side.

It did not shut properly until the person who had apparently opened it was well into the room.

"How do you do ... how do you do, Mrs Keymer?"

Mr Stephens was genial and breezy, and he looked cheerfully over the top of his pince-nez.

"May I introduce my friend Colonel Forsythe, and also my young friend Sir Nigel Peterson?"

"How do you do?" As Nigel stepped forward and held the small, weakly clinging hand, he could have sobbed with relief.

This—this, and he had expected something fierce and awful. This! This poor little quiet, faded thing with the gentle folded mouth.

Oh, Flame, Flame, how could you!

"H-m! you're her brother?" Mrs Keymer's voice was stronger than Nigel had expected it to be.

"Yes." Nigel relinquished the flaccid hand.

"H-m, then I should say that there is some excuse for Hugh."

Mrs Keymer had swung round with the quickness of a lizard and was addressing the lawyer.

"Well ..."

The lawyer did not return any further response to this remark, but he beamed cordially, and taking off his pince-nez, he swung them a little on the cord, and then put them on again.

"Well, get it over; what have you all come down for?" Mrs Keymer advanced a little farther into the room.

"Shall we just sit down and discuss it a little?" Mr. Stephens took command of the situation and waved his well-kept hand towards a chair. "That's better. Sit down Forsythe, and you too, Sir Nigel. That's it! Now then . . ."

Mr Stephens drew a little table towards him and leant over it a little with hands quietly clasped.

He smiled at Mrs Keymer.

"Get on with it! What do you want?" Mrs Keymer slipped a heel out of one of her shoes, and began to swing it on her toes.

"Since I came down here before with your husband's urgent request that you should divorce him," began Mr Stephens, speaking very quietly and calmly, "the situation has changed a little. He has now authorized me to offer you more generous terms. He is now prepared to settle two thousand a year upon you for life."

"Good God, what's making him put on the jam like that?" Mrs Keymer asked bluntly.

Mr Stephens hoisted his eyebrows up a little farther, and then, lowering them, looked quietly out through his pince-nez.

"He has received very favourable terms from America for the rights of his last book," he said.

Mrs Keymer stared for a moment or two, and then she too leant forward and spoke with horrid intuition.

"You fat old liar, he hasn't!" she said; "he's put that little slut in the family way, and he's frightened out of his senses. Good job too!"

Mrs Keymer began to laugh.

"Nigel, sit down!" Colonel Forsythe said sharply.

"She's . . ." Nigel was up on his feet and his young hands were clenching and unclenching.

"Sit down, Sir Nigel." Mr Stephens' voice came with authority.

Pale and trembling, Nigel dropped back into his chair again.

"As I was saying," Mr Stephens spoke with the utmost imperturbability, "Mr Keymer is now in a position to offer you very excellent terms, Mrs Keymer. Taking all things into consideration, I should say that you would be very well advised to accept them."

"And I say I'll see him in hell first," said Mrs Keymer, and she drew her top lip quite back this time.

"And as for you, you gutless little fool . . ." she faced Nigel, who got up, white as paper, "go back to your beastly ancestral castle, and get it ready to receive your sister with her bastard child. . . ."

"Gerald, she's not to say it!" Nigel cried out and turned from one man to another. "I'll kill her . . . I'll kill her!"

"Pull yourself together, Nigel."

Colonel Forsythe walked round the table and put an urgent hand on the heaving shoulder.

"I suppose you thought that you'd touch my heart if you brought this young thing down to intercede," Mrs Keymer said.

She thrust out her chin, and spoke in a sort of monotonous undertone.

"But you've only made it harder. Let the slut starve in the gutter; let her and her nameless brat wander round to be spat on. Let that bloody husband of mine suffer, let him suffer I tell you. . . ."

Mrs Keymer swore horribly; vile oaths dragged up from an obscene sub-consciousness.

The three men stood still. There was nothing more to be done evidently—only to get away as quickly as possible.

"And now, good day to you," went on Mrs Keymer, and she made a little bow and stood still.

"Good day." Mr Stephens was the imperturbable lawyer again, and he held out his hand.

So did Colonel Forsythe, but Nigel gripped his shaking hands together.

"No," he said, and he turned to the door.

Mrs Keymer watched them go, laughing noiselessly. As they went, she stooped to the rug.

What made Nigel turn as he held the glass door-handle in his hand he never knew. But he did, and as he did he saw what brought his heart up sick into his throat.

"Drop it, you devil!"

He was across the floor again, sending the small table flying as he came.

"No, let it burn like that dirty sister of yours."

Mrs Keymer was chuckling as she tried to force the soft furry body into the burning coals.

"Gerald, here, help, somebody!"

Nigel was shouting as he flung himself on the small, quietly dressed woman.

"Let it go, you beast—you . . ."

He had the little hard wrists in his hands and was dragging them away from the fire.

"Ah! . . ." he screamed, as something small and smelling of fire was dragged clawing down his face.

"That's spoilt your precious beauty for you!" Mrs Keymer, released, stood gasping and laughing. "Got your eye, has it? Good! Get away, you little beast!"

She flung the kitten on to the ground, where, lifting one singed paw, it limped weakly away.

"Gerald, she's put out my eye."

The two men were back in the room again,

and Nigel stood with his handkerchief to his face, trembling.

"No, no, don't; she can't have done!" Gerald Forsythe spoke like an agonized boy. "Stephens!"

But the room was suddenly full of people, and someone with a beautiful white apron was standing close to Mrs Keymer.

"Come, come, now," she was saying in a soothing voice; "come along now, that's it."

Mrs Keymer was led out of the room, still chuckling quietly.

"Bring Sir Nigel in here."

It was Mrs Unwin speaking this time.

"Mary, go quickly to Number Seven. Dr Hingely has just gone up there. Come along, Sir Nigel."

Mrs Unwin slipped her arm into the young, trembling one.

"It will be quite all right, directly you have seen the doctor. Yes, I think if you will just leave us alone, Mr Stephens, please . . ."

Dr Hingely was young and clever and reassuring. And Nigel, gripping his hands together to hear the verdict of partial blindness, began to weep with excitement and relief when he heard that there was nothing much more amiss than a badly torn lower eyelid.

"But I got the kitten away from her all right, and it was hardly hurt," he said, when, white from the pain of the surgical stitches, he lay back on the hard couch, a tumbler in his brown hands.

"Look here, I'm going to speak to you as one man to another," Dr Hingely said quietly. "And I'm not going to speak from the moral standpoint, either; that lies between a man and his God. But don't you be too hard, Sir Nigel. That has been

Hugh Keymer's life—that, the sort of thing that you have just seen."

He paused and went on.

"Remember it when you feel inclined to be bitter, as of course you do feel inclined; naturally, you're young, and a brother—I absolutely understand.

"But that's the life that a man of imagination and intellect has had to lead for the last fifteen years, and might have to lead for the next twenty. Upon my soul!"

The doctor broke off abruptly.

"Won't she die?" Nigel sat up and put the glass back on the tiled table.

"Very little chance of it." The doctor spoke bluntly as he hung the towel carefully over the rail. "But, of course, in these cases we can never tell. . . . Now, then—if you are sure you feel quite well again . . ."

He walked back to the couch and stood looking down on it.

"If only she could die before the baby is born."

Time has a way of hurling itself along when it has anything dreadful in store for you. Before you know where you are, you are deposited breathless and despairing in front of the thing that you have been trying to shut your eyes to for months and weeks.

"Now, then, let's see how you'll tackle *this!*"

Time stands aside and waits maliciously.

So it was with Hugh!

The time had come for them to leave Kashmir; *where were they to go?* He was wondering this one morning as he went plunging down through the aromatic undergrowth to have his morning bath.

Wondering is not the word; he was searching his soul in torment for an answer to the question that had haunted him day and night for months.

The only person who was not tormented was Flame. Wrapped in the shelter of a love that transcended anything that she had ever dreamed of, she was almost perfectly happy.

The only reason that she was not quite perfectly happy was that Nigel had not answered any of her letters.

"Why won't he write?"

Curled up under a beautiful moleskin rug, Flame put the question for about the fortieth time to the man who sat smoking under the standard lamp.

"Because he is angry with me, Flame, and he vents it on you because he knows that is the way to make me suffer most."

"But what is there to be so desperately angry about? Even if I had known that Mother wasn't there anymore, I should never have gone home again."

Flame hoisted herself up onto one rounded elbow.

"You might have done." Hugh's voice went suddenly hard, and he got up out of his chair.

"I never should. Hugh, Hughie . . . come over here, and let me kiss your beloved angel head."

Flame buried her mouth in the thick hair.

"Hugh, Hugh, don't, beloved! If you knew, if you only knew how I adore you, how I don't care for anything but you! Don't even let your angel hair get white Hugh, sweetheart. . . ."

Flame's voice broke.

"I feel sometimes as if I . . ."

Hugh's face was hidden in the soft neck.

"I know you do, beloved. But don't, because I only feel unspeakable joy that I belong to you."

Flame was staring out over the frosted head, her eyes heavy with tears.

Sometimes, too, unknown to the man who lay close to her heart, she suffered torments of fear. But she would have died rather than let him know it.

It was fear of the future, she felt; what was it like to have a baby? Supposing that, as a punishment, because they were not properly married, it was crippled or mad or something?

"God, God, don't let it be!" Flame would cry the words aloud in her soul.

But even as she cried them she realized the futility of them.

What was the good of crying out for mercy when you didn't mean to alter the way you were going on? If she had made up her mind to leave Hugh, then it would have been a different matter altogether. . . .

"Well, this won't do at all."

Hugh, always tenderly mindful of the girl he loved, raised his head.

"Yes, it will: it's what I like best, to have you close to me like this."

Flame's little mouth had an expression of obstinacy on it.

"Put your head down again; I'm going to tell you something. I'm going to tell you something that you've never heard before, which is, that you're the most heavenly good-looking man that was ever created."

"You little idiot!"

But Hugh's nice mouth was laughing again, which was what Flame had wanted it to be.

"Yes, you are; and that's what I can never understand . . . how you can go liking me when I look . . . so . . . stupid." Flame flushed scarlet.

"Don't, darling!" Hugh lifted his head.

"Yes, well, but I must say it. For such ages now I've been no good . . . don't you know what I mean? And yet you are so heavenly!

"Hugh, what shall I do if I die and we aren't even properly together anymore?"

And then the hidden terror leapt out, and Flame began to sob wildly.

As he tenderly comforted her, the terror and anxiety always raging in his own soul almost threatened to get Hugh down.

They must get more within range of civilization, they must get somewhere where, in the event of anything not going absolutely right, the best medical skill would be available.

But where? Under the circumstances, where?

And God, Who in spite of our hopelessness, is always watching an opportunity to help us out of the misery in which we have landed ourselves through our own stupidity, put it into Hester Lane's head to write to Hugh.

He got the letter one day when, after an English mail that brought with it no message of hope, he was very nearly at the end of his tether.

Hester had not written to Hugh without the most terrific heart-searchings. Was it right? That was the question that agitated her night and day.

"How do you mean, right?" Sir Herbert Benson smiled as he asked the question.

How this woman had altered in appearance since he had taken her to his heart.

"Well, I mean that this is a Christian Mission. Have I any right to introduce in to it a girl who . . ." And Hester stopped.

"You mean that you are afraid of her contaminating you all?"

"No, no, of course not." Hester flushed deeply.

"Well, then, what is there to be afraid of?"

"I don't know. But I can't have them both." Hester spoke hurriedly and inconsequently.

"No, no; I don't think that under the circumstances it would be at all suitable that you should," said Sir Herbert Benson.

"But he will never leave her to go through all that alone," said Hester, and then, flushing, she caught hold of the great doctor's hand and began to weep.

"My child, don't grieve over it!" Sir Herbert's eyes were tender. "Write to Keymer and offer to have Flame Peterson here, and leave the rest."

"Somehow I feel that I can't." And then Hester broke down.

"Silly child!" said Sir Herbert tenderly. "Write your letter, and I will also speak to Seymour. We might between us be able to fix up somewhere for Keymer to go; he must be a terribly unhappy man.

"But, of course, the whole thing must be kept desperately quiet, otherwise the whole station will be by the ears. Write your letter, darling, and then we will talk it over again."

So the letter was written. Hugh took it from the postman as he started out for his walk that evening.

Flame wanted some eau-de-Cologne, and Hugh was going into Srinager to get it.

But when he had read it, he sat down on a little heap of stones by the side of the road and dropped his head into his hands.

For since that morning when the English mail had come with the long letter from his lawyer, he had felt utterly hopeless.

But here was a ray of light for the immediate future, anyhow.

Flame shrank and trembled when he told her.

"I don't want to go there. She didn't like me, and I shall be afraid. Even with you there I shall be afraid. I would rather stay here and have it."

"You can't do that, darling," said Hugh quietly.

"Why can't I?" Flame trembled pitifully.

"Because I say so," said Hugh briefly.

There were some things that Flame could not be told, and one was that she was a creature outcast. And by his doing: Hugh had had his punishment.

"You ought to tell me more kindly, when I am so afraid and wretched," sobbed Flame. "It's a most frightful thing to have a baby when you are not properly married. Why, oh why did I have one?"

"Flame, don't!"

Hugh stood quite still when he had spoken. For a moment he really thought that the physical pain in his heart would crack it across.

It was true, he had brought this child to this pass himself. By his love.

Love!

He suddenly laughed hoarsely.

Flame stirred uneasily.

"I don't care for the way you're laughing, Hugh, what is the matter with you?"

But Hugh had gone with a muttered excuse. He fastened the loop of the tent across with a hand that felt oddly numb.

How Fate got her own back, he thought, stumbling stupidly out into the starlight. Flame was reproaching him now; soon she would hate him.

And he loved her, loved her, and he had brought her to this pass! A funny sort of love, he thought, beginning to laugh with broken guttural sounds.

Ten minutes afterwards, mercifully for Hugh, the laughter had changed to tears.

A little later, bitterly ashamed of himself, he crept quietly into the dressing-tent and began to dress for dinner.

Flame greeted him from the luxurious sofa with hands held out and a working mouth:

"Hugh, I was horrible ... I was horrible! It's because I don't feel well ... that's all it is. Love, I would like to go to Dr Lane, and I like having the baby ... I do indeed!"

"Sweetheart! Dearest!"

Hugh held the little head against him.

"God, get us through this time somehow, and I will try and made amends!"

He flung the prayer out wildly, not knowing that he prayed.

Chapter
Eight

It was much easier to get out of Kashmir than it had been to get out of Port Said.

Money will do most things, and this time it provided a motor, the last word in luxury, and many things to make Flame's journey more comfortable.

"Will you be able to take me to Dr Lane's?" She was clinging a little feverishly to her lover's hand.

The mail had just left the last big station before they reached Jarnagar, and Flame knew that the time of separation was drawing near.

She had promised to be brave; Hugh had told her that they could not be together for this bit of road, but that directly the baby was born and she was well again he would come and fetch her away.

"Where shall we go, then?" asked Flame, trying to speak brightly.

"Oh, to all sorts of heavenly places," replied Hugh cheerfully.

He spoke equally cheerfully, although his eyes were dark with anxiety.

"Of course I shall, darling. And you know, even though I am not actually in the same house with you, I shall be quite near. The Seymours live about a quarter of an hour's walk from the Mission."

"Having it called a Mission makes it sound so stiff," said Flame, clinging to a bit of Hugh's coat.

"But I am sure it won't be stiff," replied Hugh cheerily.

But as he spoke he shivered. The awfulness of what lay ahead of her.

For him to bring the girl he loved, a creature shamed in the eyes of everyone, to what must be her most extreme hour of anguish.

To stand himself, a man who had always been one to be reckoned with, a hateful figure of selfishness and lust.

But to his justice, Hugh did not at this crisis of his life take his own feelings much into account.

Flame's welfare was all he cared about.

He had had ghastly moments of misgiving about her capacity to weather safely what was just ahead of her, and as that was so, Hester's letter had come like a rope thrown out to a drowning man.

She was a brilliant surgeon, a brilliant everything where the physical condition of women was concerned; very well, then, she was the person to have charge of Flame at this more than awful time that was nearly on her.

The little group on the platform waiting for the mail was hardly more at its ease than the two who sat closely together in the luxurious first-class compartment.

Ann was the only one who was quite serene; she had been told all the facts of the case before it had been finally decided that the Seymours should take Hugh, and when she had heard her husband to the end, she had wrinkled up her little white forehead.

"But what's the difficulty about having him here?" she asked.

"Well, darling, you see when two people decide utterly to disregard all the laws that other people abide by, they have got to take their chance," said Tony Seymour bluntly.

"What sort of chance? ... the sort of chance of her perhaps dying in awful misery because he isn't near her, or him going through frightful agonies of wondering about her and not being able to find out because people will wonder.

"Oh, Tony! how can you? Supposing you had been married to an awful person who made you wretched, don't you suppose I would have lived with you thousands and thousands of times?"

Ann's eyes were wide and reproachful.

So it had been settled.

There they stood on the beaten-earth platform. Hester, very pale and still, but with a glow of content in her eyes that not even her immediate discomfort could quench.

Tony, tall and lean, with a cigarette between his lips; and Ann, looking like a pink rose, peeping out of her black furs, for it was seven o'clock in the evening and Jarnagar had cold weather with the nip of an early English spring in its breath.

"Shall I kiss her?" Ann spoke hastily, with a tug at the Burberry sleeve, as the long train came swinging slowly round a corner into view.

"No!"

Tony Seymour spoke decidedly and firmly; but when he saw the tiny drawn face peeping out from between furs far more costly than Ann's, he regretted his hasty decision.

It was only a child; what a brutal shame!

But Ann for the first time in her life disregarded her husband. She drew close to Flame and stared straight into her eyes.

"Why, we're rather alike," she said, "even I can see that. How do you do? How glad, how very glad I am to see you."

She leant forward and kissed the pale face.

"Do be kind to him."

Flame's eyes had begun to stream at this totally unexpected welcome. She dragged Ann a little way away from the others.

"We've never been away from each other before, and it kills me to think about it."

"Of course I will." Ann spoke sturdily and reassuringly. "Of course I will. And now, show him to me; I want to see what he's like."

And the two walked back to the three standing awkwardly under the flickering yellow lamp.

"How do you do?" Ann had Hugh's hand in hers.

"How do you do, Mrs Seymour?"

Hugh's voice was quiet, and his slightly drawn mouth did not smile.

But his heart was surging out in gratitude to this girl who had given Flame a kiss of welcome.

"I am very glad to see you indeed," said Ann. "And more than anything I shall love it when we have the baby to play with. You must both come and stay with us then.

"Now we can only have you, because of

course Miss Peterson must go somewhere else, but afterwards it will be different."

Ann beamed.

Hester broke the awful silence. Both men stood staring straight in front of them. But there was a laugh at the back of Tony's eyes.

Trust Ann to say something desperate, he thought, turning to beckon a passing luggage coolie.

"I shall come and see you every day." The little party was moving towards the wide echoing entrance to the station.

But Flame was not listening. Was she going to be torn away from her lover now? she wondered, hanging desperately back to take hold of his hand.

"Darling, you promised me you would try to be brave." Hugh returned the frantic grasp with a pressure almost as frantic.

This child of his! Oh, hadn't he expiated his sin again and again!

"Don't cry, sweetheart," he urged desperately, stooping down to look into the little face.

With a strangling, snorting cough, Flame wrenched back the sobs that were forcing their way upward. For his sake she must try; but oh, the awful misery of it!

She stumbled up into the big car that stood waiting for her and Hester. Hugh tucked the rug round their knees quietly enough.

But by the light of one of the station lamps Tony Seymour caught sight of his face: and he cleared his own throat abruptly as he turned away.

"Well, Keymer, shall we make a move?" he spoke after a little pause.

The big car with Flame and Hester in it had gone, swinging out of the station yard with a slowly diminishing tail-light.

Ann was standing very still; she too had seen the stricken face and was trying not to cry.

"Oh, thanks!"

Hugh Keymer raised his head. She had gone: sent perhaps to her death, and by him.

"Thanks very much, is it a car? Oh yes!"

"I say, you know, she'll be all right."

Tony Seymour spoke under cover of the darkness as he fumbled with the door of the car.

"No, Ann, you get in in front with me, then Mr. Keymer can stow his luggage away behind. I say, it'll all turn out all right," he spoke again, urgently this time, only conscious of an intense desire to comfort.

"Thanks very much, Seymour."

Hugh spoke quietly. She had gone, perhaps he would never see her again.

All that little soft, childish sweetness crushed out of the world by him.

By him—her lover.

Her murderer!

Hugh's breath came unevenly.

"Tony, he hasn't got in." Ann spoke in a hurried undertone.

Her husband was settling himself in the seat beside her, turning with a hand on the wheel, to back the car a little.

"Hasn't got in?" Tony Seymour twisted his head abruptly the other way. No, by Jove! there he still stood, staring in front of him.

"I say, Keymer!"

He raised his voice a little.

"Oh, I'm sorry!" Hugh Keymer laughed a little, apologetically, and stepped blindly up into the car.

Miss Harris was the one now who was most exercised about the whole thing.

Flame had settled down into it with a quiet, acquiescent acceptance. After all, there was nothing else to be done: her lover wished her to be at the Mission, so at the Mission she would be. In her heart of hearts there was a certain amount of relief about it.

Flame was afraid of the immediate future, more afraid than she had allowed Hugh to know.

As for Hugh, he was experiencing a time of relief from almost unbearable anxiety. For the last few months he had been in a constant state of terror lest something should go wrong, and he not be able instantly to get hold of a doctor to put it right.

"Didn't you think he was an old man at first? Now he's got to look quite young again."

Ann, who had quite gone down before Hugh's undeniable charm, spoke excitedly.

"Yes, he certainly looks much better."

Tony Seymour spoke non-committally, although he too was very much attracted by Hugh. The two men had become very intimate, for Hugh was passionately grateful to the Seymours for taking him in, and did not hesitate to show it.

It was all made easier by Sir Herbert Benson, who had known Hugh before, and Mrs Keymer too, and who, because of this earlier knowledge, in a sense held a brief for Hugh.

So the situation was harmonious and easy, and the three had many an excellent game of golf together, with the garrison chaplain to make a fourth.

"Had you better ask him?"

Hugh's eyes had got their tortured look back again when Tony Seymour had first made the suggestion.

"Oh yes, rather; he's a splendid fellow, one of the best," Tony Seymour spoke enthusiastically.

The suggestion of the *Padre* for a fourth had come out with all the spontaneity of the unpremeditated, but it had not been so at all.

Tony Seymour and Sir Herbert Benson had laid the whole facts of the case before him first.

"I say, how awfully sad!"

The *Padre* was a young man who had spent most of his service, up to the present, firstly in Mesopotamia, and then in Waziristan. Jarnagar was his first real Cantonment station.

"Yes, it is, desperately. Of course, I suppose one ought to feel only condemnation, but really . . ." and Sir Herbert stopped abruptly and stared down into his glass.

"Let him that is without sin . . ." The *Padre* had a way of quoting Scripture in the tenderest, most delightful manner, and both men raised their heads involuntarily.

"That's a really good man!" Sir Herbert spoke enthusiastically.

"Yes, he is; the Tommies simply adore him." Tony Seymour spoke equally enthusiastically, and then a silence fell between the two men.

Both had the affair of Flame and Hugh Keymer very much at heart, and thought of very little else.

"If only that useless woman at home would die."

Tony had spoken almost fiercely one evening

when, the English mail in, Hugh had with a gentle apology retired to his room without coming in to dinner.

"Ah! but that's just exactly what she won't do!"

Sir Herbert took the long slender pipe out of his mouth and stared into the glowing bowl of it.

"It's a disgraceful state of affairs that insanity and hopeless intemperance; both ought to be made sufficient cause for divorce."

"Ah well, but you must remember that we've got a reputation for sanctity to keep up, deserved or undeserved," said Tony Seymour, getting up and laughing ruefully.

"Anyhow, we ourselves can do a certain amount now to make the poor fellow's life a little more bearable.

"Up to the present he's simply had to stick in the compound for fear of being seen. But now, we four can clear off to the links. The *Padre* won't say a word, and no one will notice him out there."

But Miss Harris, one of the small-souled of this earth, did not take things quite so quietly.

"Who is she? That's what I want to know!" she said one day to Hilly, jerking the question at her, as she sat at her writing-table correcting exercise books.

"Who is she? Why, she's an old friend of Dr Lane's."

"Yes, but old friends of people don't come out to India to have their babies. And they don't come to Missions either, when they can afford to dress as Mrs Peterson does. Where's her husband? That's what *I* want to know!" finished Miss Harris firmly.

"Where could he be? In his own station, I expect."

"Well, I think it's odd. I don't think it's right. We're all fellow-workers in the Mission field, and Mrs Peterson's underclothes are not the underclothes of a Christian woman."

"How do you know?" Hilly's good-tempered face was creased with curiosity.

"Why, I took her in her breakfast the other day," said Miss Harris. "And her nightdress, and the *peignoir* she wore over it, just a mass of filet lace. And her hand. Well, of course, to my mind, that settled it; just a tiny little strip of silver on it.

"Well, you and I know what a wedding-ring should be, and that wasn't one," finished Miss Harris, to whom a wedding-ring began and ended in a quarter of an inch of pinkish gold.

"There was a young married woman on the ship I came out in who had a ring like that," said Miss Hill shyly. "It's platinum, the very latest."

Hilly hated to think the worst of anyone, and to think that the Mission sheltered a young woman on the eve of motherhood who was not even married was surely the very worst you could think of anyone.

But Miss Harris only sucked the end of her darning cotton and sniffed. The wonderful cherished beloved look of this golden-headed child roused her deepest ire.

That wasn't the look of the ordinary married woman at all!

Miss Harris had heaps of sisters-in-law, and she had seen them going to have babies too. This was sin, and Miss Harris was going to find out about it.

And the Devil played into her hands, for she bumped into Mrs Holroyd-Browne, who was only too willing to tell her all she knew about Flame.

Flame was alone when Miss Harris got back.

It was about half-past eleven, and Hester, very tall and slim in a white overall, was stooping, brows a little drawn, under the great plate-glass window of the operating theatre.

Miss Hill was in the school. The buzz of droning voices came faintly to Flame through the sunlight.

"Oh, I say, Miss Harris, how you made me jump!"

Flame turned from the foot of the long cane chair on which she was laying her workbasket and a bundle of soft, lacy little garments.

She always enjoyed these long mornings of sewing; such heavenly little things; little fat coats with necks that would only do for a big doll.

"Put down those emblems of your shame," said Miss Harris.

She had been fairly sure that she would catch Flame like this, and had been practising what she would say.

"How do you mean?" Flame turned with a whitening face.

"What I say. Put down those shameful things."

"All right," and Flame let the soft bundle drop on to the end of the chair.

One little white coat fell away from the others and lay by itself on the matting. Flame saw it, and wondered if she should pick it up.

It was her first attempt at knitting; she and Hugh had pored over the directions together.

When she had got hopelessly muddled in making the sleeve, he had seized the wool and the needles and said that he knew he could do it much better himself.

"But you've made such a weeny cuff!" Flame was in convulsions of laughter as he brought it to show her.

"It's got to be weeny!" Hugh's eyes were alight.

"But not as weeny as *that!*"

Flame had thought of the little tiny hand with the tinier fingers that would be crammed through it, and she had choked, and clung to her lover.

"It'll be ours, won't it? Like nothing else could be," she breathed.

"Yes, it will, darling."

Hugh's voice was as it always was when he spoke to Flame, full of cheer.

But his eyes were as they always were when Flame could not see them, full of despair.

But Miss Harris did not know all this; and if she had done, it would only have stiffened her resolution to make Flame suffer more.

So that when she saw her movement to retrieve the little coat, she stepped quickly forward and put her foot on it.

"Don't! You'll make it all dirty!" Flame cried out, and tried to stoop quickly.

But Miss Harris had already got it safely under her foot; and then she too stooped and dragged it out from under her shoe.

"Mind the *cuff!*"

The tears had begun to stream down Flame's face. Her most precious thing!

"Give it to me; it's the thing I like best; my husband made it, at least, a bit of it; give it to *me!*"

Flame made a lunge forward.

"Your husband! You woman of sin and shame, you have no husband!"

Flame let her outstretched hands tremble slowly to her sides.

"How do you know?" she said in a dreadful whisper.

"Never mind how I know; take it from me that I know," said Miss Harris.

"And when I see you there in your costly wrappings, with your sewing in your lap, knitting for the little lamb that is only to come into this world to be a thing of sin and shame, I could weep. Oh, you wicked, wicked woman, you!"

"How do you mean, a thing of sin and shame? How can anyone be that for what they haven't done themselves?"

Flame's eyes were wide and her lips were suddenly stiff. This was something new.

She had grasped for some time that she and Hugh had done a wrong thing in living together without being married, but that this should affect the baby!

"How can you be that?" she repeated.

"Easily," said Miss Harris. "God in His infinite love and mercy has ordained it thus. Your child will be a thing of shame; it can never be baptized."

"But does that matter very much?" asked Flame with quivering lips.

"Matter?" said Miss Harris, staring speechlessly.

"Well, but after all, if God has that sort of a

plan that something that can't help being born is, and then is punished for it, it rather turns you against things like baptism," said Flame, trembling.

"It's like having a party and not letting a child in because it's not properly dressed, when it's its parents fault that it isn't.

"Besides, if the baby isn't God's already, how can just being baptized make it His? Heaps of people don't believe in baptism, Quakers for instance.

"What happens to all of them?" asked Flame, suddenly interested, and forgetting the sudden terror she had gone through at hearing that the baby would be a thing of shame.

"Hell fire for the unbeliever," said Miss Harris firmly; "that little child of yours, if it is born alive, which God forbid! will go through life a little marked soul. If it dies before birth, and may God in His infinite mercy ordain it thus, it will—"

"No, no!"

Flame flung herself forward.

"No, no, don't say it . . . because it is alive . . . it is alive! And if it dies now, it hasn't a chance . . . it hasn't a chance! Don't you see, if it's even just born I could sort of see it, and plead with God for it, but if it does first . . . Hugh! Hugh!"

Flame began to scream.

"Don't take that name of shame upon your lips," said Miss Harris.

She did not realize that screams from her meant a good deal more than screams from one of her own sisters-in-law.

"Pray to your God that in His infinite mercy He may—"

"But what have I got to pray about?"

Flame had got her clenched hands up close to her mouth and was staring over them.

"The baby's there, it's too late! Because either way, you say it hasn't a chance! Hugh, Hugh! Why did you let me have one? Hugh! Hughie!"

And Flame, gathering her soft draperies round her, began to stumble blindly up and down the verandah.

But this last remark was altogether too much for Miss Harris.

The big bell over the arched doorway into the school was beginning to boom out the hour of twelve.

So she turned to go. And as she turned, Flame made one little desperate rush towards her.

"Say that perhaps you've got it wrong," she gasped; "after all, no one, even a missionary, can know everything for certain about God. Say that perhaps there is a chance for it. Otherwise, I don't know . . ."

Flame stopped, and suddenly an odd expression came into her eyes.

But Flame's last cry to her lover had turned all Miss Harris' starved instincts into a flaming fiery furnace of jealousy.

"Don't touch me," she said hardly.

"Then of course I must," said Flame; "if it's as bad as that. Besides, anyhow, how could I let it wander about alone when it wasn't its fault, I must go with it, Hughie! Darling, darling Hughie . . ."

Flame made another two or three steps towards the edge of the matted verandah, and before Miss Harris could prevent her, she was over the edge of it and down on the gravel below.

"Why did you do that?"

Miss Harris, demented with fright, was also down on the gravel, kneeling by Flame's side.

"Because I don't care for the idea of it being alone with God," said Flame, with funny twisted blue lips. "And nobody can fall over a verandah, when they are going to have a baby, without dying. At least, I hope they can't. Hughie . . . Hughie!"

Flame's head rolled a little over on to one side.

Miss Harris was up and galloping like a hunted rat towards the hospital.

Death, or the messenger of Death. There was something in the sound of the padding bare feet coming nearer and nearer through the darkness that told Hugh so without a doubt.

He gripped the stem of his wineglass as the blood fled back from his heart in a ghastly tide.

The *Padre*, who with his elbows on the table was listening cheerfully to rather a long story of Sir Herbert Benson's, saw the whitening knuckles, and although still listening, shifted his gaze a little.

"*Burra doctor-sahib hain?*" Simon, the Mission chuprassie, was not as young as he had been, and the words came gaspingly from the back verandah.

"*Hain!*" But Francis, the Seymours' Goanese butler, spoke with a certain amount of reserve.

His master and mistress were dining out, certainly, but it was not the thing to rush into one person's bungalow and immediately ask for another.

"*Hain,*" he repeated in the vernacular; "but the three Sahibs drink the port wine: wait!"

"*Attcha!*" and Simon sank down on the wide

flagged space with almost an audible creaking of his old bones.

But Hugh sent back his chair with a shove: "I say, Benson, I think you're wanted. Excuse my interrupting, but . . ."

"Wanted? Where?" Sir Herbert stared vaguely up at the greying face on the other side of the table. "Oh, I see—excuse me, will you?"

He took the note from the servant at his elbow.

"H-m . . ." Reading, he got slowly up on to his feet, and being a very great doctor, his face did not change. "H-m—well, you two won't mind being left alone for a little while, I expect . . ." and slipping the note into his pocket, Sir Herbert went out.

"Something is wrong with . . ." and then Hugh dropped his head into his hands with a groan.

Heart of his heart, and yet he had no name to give her!

"I hope not!" The *Padre's* chubby face was furrowed with instant sympathy.

"There is! Find out, for God's sake: I must know!" Hugh lifted haggard eyes.

"I will, of course!"

The *Padre* laid his creased table napkin down on the table, and got up.

"I say . . ." he was out on the verandah, speaking in an undertone: "I say, Benson, Keymer is in a fearful state, thinking that there is something wrong with Miss Peterson. What am I to tell him?"

"Tell him that there is: it's useless to try and keep it from him: Miss Peterson has had an accident—a fall of some kind—and Dr Lane has sent for me."

Sir Herbert Benson was shrugging himself into a Burberry and he spoke abruptly.

"But for God's sake, *Padre,* keep Keymer
here: he can do nothing at the Mission, and he'll
only hang about and drive us all frantic. We'll send
for him if it's necessary: thank Heaven, I kept my
tonga!"

Sir Herbert Benson, hands in pockets, was gone
at a dive down the two shallow stone steps,
running like a hare towards the two faintly seen
lights beyond the white gateposts.

"Well?" Hugh's voice was one agonized ques-
tioning, as after just a second's pause the *Padre*
walked back into the circle of rose-coloured light.

"Come into the drawing-room, Keymer, and
I'll tell you. Miss Peterson is very ill," he said.
"She has had some sort of a fall, and Dr Lane has
sent for Sir Herbert to help her."

"She is going to die."

Hugh was standing by a little table covered
with brass, and everything on it suddenly began to
rattle.

"No, no, she is not. Don't!" The *Padre* took
a step forward.

"She is! And I have killed her. What a score
for this God of yours!"

Hugh swung round and began to walk about,
his hands clenched over his ears.

"Keymer, don't!" The *Padre* followed him.
"To begin with, you don't know yet that Miss
Peterson is even in extreme danger. Apparently
there were no details in the note that came."

"I must go," Hugh said; "she might want me."
He started swiftly for the door.

"No, don't! Stay here!" The *Padre* got up
quickly and followed him.

"She might want me."

Hugh was talking to himself, and was already, bareheaded, halfway down the drive.

At the high white gate at the end of the avenue of trees, the *Padre* stopped short.

"Let me go on alone from here, Keymer," he urged.

"No." Hugh's voice was almost entirely without expression.

"I say, do!" the *Padre* spoke urgently, like a boy.

"No." It only came quietly again, and the *Padre*, with a little imperceptible shrug of his shoulders, fell into step by the side of the taller man.

The avenue was long and winding.

From the last turn in it you could see the Mission bungalow, a bungalow entirely in darkness, except for two rooms at the end of it, which were a blaze of light.

"Every lamp you can spare, please, Miss Hill; and then will you two go over and sleep in the hospital?" Hester, very tall and grave in her white uniform, had walked back into the big room in which Miriam kept watch.

"No," and Hugh walked on again.

Then he stopped dead, like a man with a bullet through his brain, as the shriek came echoing through the darkness.

"No, no, I can't . . . Hugh, Hugh!"

It was a cry from someone in most extreme torture.

The *Padre* always played halfback in the regimental footer team, so he was in excellent training. And he needed to be, for Hugh was a very powerful man.

"Look here, Keymer—pull yourself together." It came in staccato gasps.

"Let me go—she wants me!" Hugh was fighting like a blinded man.

"Yes, but don't you see, it's so utterly useless. They won't let you go in, and you'll only—besides, everything that can possibly be done is being done; both are there; Keymer, don't," for Hugh had groaned, very dreadfully.

"She wants me, God, and I can't go to her!"

Hugh let his head fall forward on his chest like a man wounded to death.

"Come back—we'll talk—there was some sort of a seat." The *Padre* was breathing heavily as he led Hugh back along the way they had come.

Out of earshot, he dragged Hugh along in a panic.

Across the narrow bed in the brilliantly lighted room two pairs of clever eyes met.

"What do you think?"

There was a question in Hester's eyes.

Sir Herbert shrugged his shoulders very slightly. Then he glanced down and his eyes were suddenly dark with pity.

"Chance it," he said; "it's a risk, but still . . ." The sickly clinging smell of choloroform stole through the room, and old Miriam gripped her wrinkled hands together in relief.

For Flame reminded her of the missy-baby she had nursed long years ago, the little golden-hair missy-baba of the Collector-sahib, who had loved her, and kissed her brown cheek. Miriam shed a quiet tear as she moved quietly and skilfully about the room.

On the tumbledown seat the *Padre* spoke first.

There was something in the way Hugh was sitting that tore his heart with a longing to comfort.

Hugh was sitting bolt upright, staring straight in front of him, his hands hanging down at his sides.

Listening, the *Padre* knew he was, and in a panic lest there should be something to hear, he spoke.

"Keymer, I wish you would tell me . . ."

He stopped and Hugh turned his head.

"Tell you what?" he said.

The *Padre* winced at the withered voice through the darkness.

"Well . . ." The *Padre* hesitated.

Hugh broke in:

"You mean that you wish I would blab out my penitence for the past. No, thanks! I prefer to take this last torture standing up."

"I don't mean that in the least." The *Padre* spoke without the faintest resentment in his voice "All I mean is, that sometimes when one is very near the end of one's tether, to confide in someone helps. Perhaps you do not feel like that. Don't think for one moment . . ."

"No, I know—forgive me." Hugh's response was instant, and he flung out his hands. "It's just that: *Padre,* if she dies, I have killed her!"

Hugh was up on his feet again, the whitening knuckles showing plainly through the darkness.

The *Padre* drew him quietly down again onto the seat.

"Look here, Keymer, in saying that, you are unreasonable. I don't know in the least the circumstances that led up to this affair, but this I do know . . ."

"You don't know—how can you know? She

was a child, and innocent, and hadn't a ghost of a chance with me when I—God, God, if she dies! *Padre, Padre!*"

Hugh's head was down on his wrenched hands again.

The *Padre* waited a little while, and then with a frantic prayer that he might not say too much, he began to speak.

Hugh listened; at first apathetically, and then with a growing consciousness of the real goodness of the man beside him.

"But you know, Keymer," the *Padre* was still speaking, "I cannot believe that you took this step without some very grave provocation from somewhere. I know I ought not to appear to condone, and I don't.

"But tell me, if you can, just a little of what led up to it. You owe it to yourself. So far, I have only heard your passionate condemnation of yourself—there must be another side."

"So far as Miss Peterson is concerned, there is no other side," said Hugh quietly.

"No—quite: but, assuming that, there must be something. Your home: your home life: a man doesn't chuck that all overboard, at least a man of your type doesn't, without some very grave provocation."

The *Padre* was trying to see Hugh's face through the darkness.

"I had a certain amount of provocation, certainly." Hugh spoke slowly. "If I enlighten you a little about it, *Padre,* it is only that I feel I owe it to you. I am not whining or asking for mercy. Although if God . . ."

Hugh lifted his bleached face to the sky again.

Then out it came, the whole sordid story.

Far more sordid than anyone had any idea of —for Hugh, with the pride of the proud man who has made a fool of himself, and who has been told beforehand that he is making a fool of himself, had made desperate efforts that no one should know the true facts about his marriage.

And no one did know them; a few people knew that Mrs Keymer drank, but beyond that they knew nothing.

When he had gone so far, Hugh got up, and with the trembling gesture of a hand drawn across a wet forehead, he laughed shakily.

"You see, *Padre*," he said, "I was too proud to take my freedom when I might have had it. But I was not too proud to take the girl I loved, and drag her through the mud."

Hugh broke down again.

They talked until the crescent moon had sailed very high in the sky. The *Padre* was accustomed to dealing with men, and he knew exactly how to do it.

Nothing feeble: no impracticable code of morality impossible in a workaday world: but just this. You owe a duty to the community which you cannot afford to disregard.

"Then you mean that if she lives, I ought to leave her." Hugh jerked up his head, and his lips were white.

"Yes, I do." The *Padre* spoke quietly. "You see, Keymer, I know perfectly well that in your case things are different, you love—both of you— and in God's sight that is marriage. But by itself it isn't enough. There are certain laws for the regulation of this world that we must abide by:

otherwise, what would it be?—absolute chaos. . . ."

And then the *Padre* suddenly stopped abruptly. Running feet again, coming out of the darkness. . . .

"Oh, my God!" Hugh had stumbled up onto his feet.

"Padre-sahib mangta." Simon, the chuprassie, was padding breathlessly past them.

"Here I am!" The *Padre* spoke in English, and flung out his hand. "Stop, Simon; it's all right. Keymer, you wait here for me."

"She's dying!" Hugh was standing very still.

"No, no!" The *Padre* laid his hand on the black coat-sleeve.

"She is, and I have killed her. Go, *Padre:* don't wait. But if—don't let them keep me away from her—she will want me. . . ."

Hugh broke away from that kind hand with an awful sob. And the *Padre* started to run.

"No, no, Lord! No, not this!" As he ran he prayed. "You stop it somehow: You can; You shall!"

Flame was lying very still when the *Padre* walked into the darkened room. No more blazing light now; only one tall lamp at the head of the bed, shedding a quiet circle of light onto the big pillow.

"We can't possibly save her; her heart is giving out."

Hester had been crying as she met the *Padre* at the door.

"It's so pathetic to hear her, too: I can't think what it is that is on her mind. Mr Keymer must not come; it would break his heart, and it would be utterly useless, as she is quite unconscious. Yes, the little creature hadn't a chance from the first." This in answer to a quiet question.

"Can you leave me alone with her for a little while?" The *Padre* had his eyes on the little bed in the distance.

"Yes, that is, if you will keep Miriam. It would not be safe to leave you quite alone with her."

"Leave her to me—and Miriam. And you go and look after that man of yours.

"He will want a drink, and he will want you with him while he has it." The *Padre* spoke in a quiet, very gentle voice. "Now then, and I will send for you the instant I think it is necessary."

The *Padre* came farther into the room and stood for an instant with his chin sunk onto his chest.

"Miriam's darling say a little prayer," said Miriam, feeling that this was being a very great occasion indeed.

"I don't want to pray." Flame's voice was faint. "I want to die, to get away from cruel rats with stabbing teeth."

The *Padre* had gone quietly on his knees beside the narrow bed, and he put out one hand and laid it very gently on the little head.

"You want to live," he said, "for the sake of the man who loves you."

"No ... no ... because it is alone. Wandering, wandering, and not because of its own fault. If it could have waited ... to be baptized, I would have asked God ..."

Flame made a little fragile wailing sound, infinitely pathetic.

"Foolish little child!" The *Padre*'s voice was

very quiet and gentle, and full of kindness. "Foolish little child! You've got it all wrong, Flame. God is Love! Do you understand what I say? *Love!*"

"Love is Hughie," said Flame, and the white eyelids sank a little lower over the dark circles under them.

"Sahib!" Miriam's old eyes were on the tiny wandering fingers.

The *Padre*'s gesture was imperative, and the old woman sank back, crouching onto her heels again.

"Love is Hughie," he said, and he spoke very slowly and clearly. "Love is Hughie: I know it is, Flame. But it is something else as well. Love is God—God. Who is here beside you now. Can you hear me?"

"Yes," said Flame, and very slowly she opened her eyes again.

"Well then, listen. Just take hold of my hand and listen. God is here, and He wants you to stay here too. He will take care of your baby—far, far better than you could."

"Not punish it?" Flame's eyes were fixed very dimly on the clear ones looking into hers.

The *Padre* laughed. Such a little gentle, amused laugh.

"Flame, God is Love. You didn't understand—*Love!* How could Love do anything unjust and cruel like that? You couldn't, I couldn't . . ."

"Hughie couldn't!" and the white lips suddenly wavered a little upwards.

"No, well then, if Hughie couldn't . . ."

The *Padre* suddenly stopped speaking, because Flame's eyes were wider open and staring past him.

"Is that God just behind you?" she asked, and there was a flood of returning life in her voice.

"Yes," said the *Padre*, and he let his head drop quietly down into the blankets.

"I like the look of Him." Flame sighed comfortably. "Look, Miriam, another Sahib, just there behind this one. Lord, take hold of my hand."

Flame turned quietly onto her side.

Tony Seymour sighed. This was being darned unpleasant, no doubt about it. Right, of course, look at it how you would, but still, and Tony went on with his dressing.

He lived it all over again in his mind. The awful strained tenseness of the last week.

For one evening Hugh had come to him as he lay stretched in a long chair out under the stars, and had told him that he was going to leave the station almost at once.

"But what about Miss Peterson?"

Tony had got quietly up, his smouldering cheroot held between his thumb and forefinger.

"She stays with Dr Lane for the present." Hugh had a dreadful bleached pallor on his face, and in deepest pity the tall Sapper averted his eyes.

"But . . ." Hugh had interrupted in a sort of fierce undertone.

"Don't, Seymour, there is no question about it. It's the right thing to do, I know it now. And if it kills me—well, I have asked for it. She is young, and after a bit . . ."

Hugh had broken down, and as Tony moved again between his dressing-table and wash-hand stand, his own eyes stung again with tears.

"Why couldn't that cursed creature at home

die!" he thought as he adjusted his tie carefully to the collar.

There had been that one wild hope of the foreign telegram, too.

Hugh had brought it to him, shaking, and Tony had torn the narrow white Eastern Telegraph envelope across in a sudden gust of joyful expectation. But it had only been some futile query from Hugh's publisher.

"Oh, my sainted aunt! I can't stand much more of it."

Tony spoke in a resentful undertone, as, after reaching up for his soft hat—five A.M., no need for a *topi* yet—he tiptoed through the big bedroom in which Ann still lay sleeping.

Poor Ann! who had cried herself to sleep the night before.

"Up to the very last I thought it was going to be like Abraham and Isaac," she sobbed, "and now you see, it isn't. There isn't any more time now: I think God is very cruel."

Although Tony had never had any hope of it being like Abraham and Isaac, even he felt uncommonly wretched as he met the eyes of the man already out and waiting on the verandah.

"Hallo!" Hugh's face was grey.

"Hallo!" but after the stupid interjection Tony Seymour turned away. "I'll just get along to the garage."

He walked quickly down the two steps that led from the verandah into the compound.

"Oh, my God, much more of this I can't stand!" he said to himself as he strode along, his hands dug deep into his pockets.

Mercifully he did not have to: Ann had been

right. For as he stood stooping over the open bonnet of the car, some little adjustment of the wiring needed, Hugh was beside him again.

"Open it: I can't!" he said hoarsely, and he thrust the crumpled envelope into the jumble of wires and tappets.

Tony withdrew an oily hand with deliberation.

"I don't suppose it's anything, Keymer," he said quietly: "we always get a stack of telegrams here: let's come to the light. . . ."

But as he walked to the door of the garage, his own hands were shaking. Dash the cup of hope again from this man's lips, in this his most extreme hour of anguish, he could not.

What cursed fool had had the imbecility to send an official wire at this hour of the morning?

He tore the narrow white envelope across, and gradually the badly written words straightened themselves out in front of his eyes, and he walked back again:

"Keymer!" he said. "It is—it's your . . . your wife. She's—Keymer—it's freedom."

Chapter
Nine

(For the Reader Who Wants to
Know Exactly What Happens
to Everyone)

Late afternoon this time, and rain. Rain blurring the windows of the big car with its wild whipping.

Rain that formed big blobs like tears, and ran down the bevelled sheets and lost themselves in the grooving.

"Oh, how it's simply deluging!"

Flame shivered.

"Never mind, darling." Hugh held the small hand a little tighter.

"Yes, I know . . . but it's a sort of omen. If Nigel isn't kind to you . . . Hughie!"

Flame's mouth was set in a little straight line.

"He will be."

Hugh Keymer spoke very quietly and certainly, for Flame must never know the torment of apprehension that was turning him cold and sick.

183

To confront Flame's brother, the thought was almost more than he could stand.

"But supposing he isn't!"

The car turned in at the great gate, and began to creep slowly upwards. Flame had her face pressed against the window-pane.

"Hughie, it's just the *same!*" She flung round and buried her face in the rough overcoat sleeve.

The car crept slowly to a standstill under the wide stone porch and stood there throbbing; and there was Waterton, with Robert behind him, coming down the shallow steps.

Waterton, with just the same old mastiff face with shaking jowls, for the old butler was making no attempt to conceal the tears that were streaming down his face.

His little lamb back again, and with a husband too! For Waterton had been kept in outer darkness as to the events of the past year.

"Where is Nigel?"

Flame had her hand gripped in the old butler's.

"In the library, Miss Flame."

Waterton was looking over the little fur cap up into the face that towered above it. A good face, that—his darling had chosen well.

"No, let me go in first, my sweet."

Hugh had taken off his hat and was surrendering his overcoat to the attentive Robert.

"You wait here, Flame. Waterton, just show me which is the library, will you, please?"

"Certainly, sir." The two disappeared quietly down the long flagged hall. "Mr Keymer, Sir Nigel!"

Waterton generally called Nigel "Master Nigel," but this was being an occasion.

Hugh stood with his back to the closed door,

and faced the young figure standing with his hands nervously gripped behind him.

Nigel had in imagination rehearsed this scene many times. The man who had practically betrayed his sister—he would say . . .

And then the words died on his lips as through the lately opened door the wintry smell of chrysanthemums crept in.

Chrysanthemums, and another day in late autumn.

Chrysanthemums, the smell of them mingling with another smell, the smell of fire!

Fire, and a small clawing body being drawn whimpering down his face.

Nigel, choking, was across the polished boards in a flurry of young welcoming feet:

"Keymer, I say—I'm awfully glad . . .!" he stammered.

ABOUT THE EDITOR

BARBARA CARTLAND, the world's most famous romantic novelist, who is also an historian, playwright, lecturer, political speaker and television personality, has now written over 200 books. She has also had many historical works published and has written four autobiographies as well as the biographies of her mother and that of her brother Ronald Cartland, who was the first Member of Parliament to be killed in the last war. This book has a preface by Sir Winston Churchill. Barbara Cartland has sold 80 million books over the world, more than half of these in the U.S.A. She broke the world record in 1975 by writing twenty books in a year, and her own record in 1976 with twenty-one. In private life, Barbara Cartland, who is a Dame of the Order of St. John of Jerusalem, has fought for better conditions and salaries for Midwives and Nurses. As President of the Royal College of Midwives (Hertfordshire Branch), she has been invested with the first Badge of Office ever given in Great Britain, which was subscribed to by the Midwives themselves. She has also championed the cause for old people and founded the first Romany Gypsy Camp in the world. Barbara Cartland is deeply interested in Vitamin Therapy and is President of the British National Association for Health.